PRAISE FOR *EULOGY*

"A heartfelt novel about a son's search for the truth about his seemingly ordinary father's hidden life, *Eulogy* is achingly bittersweet. As he begins asking questions he isn't sure he wants to know the answers to, the son is forced to reassess everything he believes about the people he loves—and ultimately examine his own life choices and decisions. Quietly observed and richly absorbing."

— Christina Baker Kline, author of the #1 New York Times bestseller *Orphan Train*

"At the heart of this tender, engrossing novel are a father's secrets, a son's attempts to unearth them, and the son's struggle to understand why so much was kept hidden from him. Absorbing and perceptive."

— Jane Bernstein, author of *The Face Tells the Secret*

EULOGY

Michael Laser

Regal House Publishing

Published by
Regal House Publishing, LLC
Raleigh, NC 27587
All rights reserved

ISBN -13 (paperback): 9781646032440
ISBN -13 (epub): 9781646032457
Library of Congress Control Number: 2021943781

Interior layout by Lafayette & Greene
Cover design © by C.B. Royal
Cover image © Shutterstock/Aleshyn_Andrei

Regal House Publishing, LLC
https://regalhousepublishing.com

Printed in the United States of America

For my father

1

My father had a sweet, crooked smile that made him seem shyer than he really was. In almost every picture, he looks as if someone just told him a joke about a rabbi and a hooker. He's wearing that half-embarrassed smile in the little black-and-white photo in my hand. But who's the girl snuggling against him? Black-haired, slightly buck-toothed (like him), she leans against his shoulder but seems worried. *Con amore, Silvia*, she wrote on the back in unsteady script, the ink translucent blue. He's wearing a clean khaki uniform, and is still as thin as young Frank Sinatra—no sign of the belly to come. *Rome, July 1945*, he printed under her name. That was the year he came home and married Mom, after an engagement prolonged by the war. He's so inconceivably young here: ten years younger than my younger son. I wonder if he broke Silvia's heart.

This morning, I delivered his eulogy. An hour later, we dropped handfuls of dirt on his casket. And just now, at his kitchen table, I discovered that he kept secrets. My cheerful, well-liked, hardworking father spent three years in prison.

As a boy, I wanted to believe that he had once been heroic. He'd fought in the war, but all I ever saw him do was go to work, wash the dishes after dinner, and develop pictures in the bathroom. My friend Barry sometimes bragged about the Silver Star his father had won at Leyte, in the Pacific, for crawling up to a Jap pillbox and throwing grenades in. (His words, not mine.) My father rarely told war stories, and only one of them involved bloodshed. When I shared that one with Barry, I tacked on a more dramatic ending. Digging Dad's Purple Heart out of the linen closet, I explained that, after he was shot, he held his breath and played dead while a German soldier pried off the silver ring my mother had given him. That much was true.

But in my revised version, he shot the enemy soldier, crawled through the mud, and took his ring back.

The chapel was pleasantly cool. Sunlight spilled through the vertical blinds onto the side pews, but the Florida heat didn't penetrate. A folded flag in a clear triangular pouch balanced on the rounded lid of the casket. Two stained glass windows showed Moses bringing his people the Tablets of the Law; the windows themselves echoed the shape of the tablets. The young rabbi wore his hair slicked back like a car salesman. Though he had never met Dad, he recited the key facts with conviction, as if they'd been friends for years.

I had written a eulogy on the plane. My father's life has always struck me as epic in scope—the Depression, the war, his three careers and two wives—and I found it surprisingly comfortable to stand at the lectern and share these stories with his many friends and relatives. What I hadn't anticipated was the stone in my throat. I've been preparing myself for his death for six years, ever since his first stroke, but I had to stop twice and recover the ability to speak.

"My father may have been the happiest man I ever met. What makes this interesting is that he went through so much that could have embittered him. Childhood poverty. A war and a near-fatal wound. His wife's premature death. Two strokes. But I only saw him angry two or three times, and never heard him speak a resentful word.

"Many of you already know the stories I'm going to tell. But I'd like to honor him by remembering his life, together with all of you.

"He grew up in Williamsburg, back when only poor people lived there. My grandparents had a fruit stand and my grand-father gave music lessons, but they couldn't afford to feed themselves and their children. My father spent a lot of time across the hall, with the Abneys—a 'colored' family, as he called them—who fed him and welcomed him to their parties, where he learned to dance. With his brother Sam, he explored the tunnels of the new subway line before the tracks were laid. Hot sweet potatoes cost five cents, he once told me. You'd break one in half and share it with a brother or sister. Then you'd suck it to get every last bit. That's everything I know about his childhood.

"A neighbor helped get him a job making rosaries at a little shop called Muller's. (When people said, 'You made what?' he would shrug and explain, 'I needed a paycheck.') He took pride in his craftsmanship. I loved watching him twist wire with his needle-nose pliers: his skill amazed me. The store was on Barclay Street, around the corner from the Woolworth Building, and the nuns who came in were fond of him. They may have assumed he was Italian; he always looked Italian to me. When he was recovering from his wounds in an army hospital, a novena was said for him. I finally looked up what that means: nine days of prayer. I'm guessing few Jews have received the honor.

"He enlisted in 1943, as soon as he turned eighteen. But he didn't want to marry my mother until he came home, in case 'something happened.'"

(My draft included the tale of the German soldier and the ring. I left it out because I didn't want people to think of him that way: so powerless that his only recourse was to play dead.)

"Dad loved to tell stories, but not war stories. I only know a couple.

"They gave him an IQ test and he did well. An officer asked him, 'How would you like to serve in the Air Corps, soldier?' Dad answered, 'I don't think I'd like to jump out of a plane.' The officer said, 'I didn't ask you that.' Next thing he knew, the guy had angrily stamped his papers with the word *Infantry*—the most dangerous place you could be.

"One other army story. Ten minutes before he got shot, he said to his friend Fred, 'These mountains would be a terrible place to get hit. They'd never find you.' And they didn't find him for twenty-four hours. He had sulfa drugs in his pack, and he took more than you were supposed to, to ward off infection."

(He *peed blood*, I had written, but I left that unsaid.)

"The war affected him more than he wanted us to know.

Once when he was napping, I went over and blew on his hand as a prank. He jumped and put both hands out toward me, as if I were an attacker he had to strangle. Then he apologized and told me never to do that again. I didn't.

"Making rosaries paid too little to support a family, so he took the civil service test and got a job boxing mail at the General Post Office in downtown Brooklyn. My mother helped him by quizzing him on the postal codes for upstate New York.

"The post office transferred him upstate for a few years, just before I was born. My first memory is the day he came back. I was three and didn't know him. Paul and Holly ran to him, but I hung back as he hugged them. He cried, and that scared me."

(My aunts and uncles and my father's friends must have considered me a naïve fool: a sixty-one-year-old man who still believed the fairy tale he'd been told in childhood, that the post office had transferred his father upstate for three years.)

"His friend Fred Stapleton called one day, wildly excited, because he'd just found out that my father had survived the war. 'I thought you were dead,' he said. 'I saw you go down.' One thing led to another, and they ended up working together as exterminators in Johnson City, New York. This time, we all went with him.

"Fred was a good man, Dad always said. They got along well, even though Fred and his wife were devout Christians who believed that Jews couldn't go to heaven.

"My mother missed her family, so we moved back to Queens when I was six, and Dad started an exterminating business of his own. Once I was big enough to help, he took me along sometimes as an assistant, and seemed happy to have me with him. (*Silent Spring* had come out a few years before, but exterminators hadn't gotten the message yet.) One afternoon we visited a diner that had waited too long to deal with its roach problem. When Dad started spraying, bugs rained down on him from the ceiling. They ran around on his shirt and pants while I whisked them away with a napkin. That's the only time I ever heard him curse.

"He was the kind of father who did funny tricks for his kids—like pretending to break his own nose, or letting us pull his finger off, or washing his glass eye in his mouth and putting it back in. (Did I startle you? Like I said, it was just pretend.) Jumping ahead thirty years, few things have made me happier than watching Dad do those same tricks for my sons.

"Every summer, we visited Uncle Sam on Long Island, and swam in his above-ground pool. My parents made me put my pajamas on before we left. I fell asleep in the car every time; Dad carried me into the house and put me in bed. The jostling would always wake me, and I'd see his face above mine in the dark."

(That was the first pause. I could see it so clearly. My body remained in the chapel, but my soul was seven again.)

"On Saturday nights, we all watched *Gunsmoke* together. We would act out the gunfight during the opening credits. We took turns, Paul or Holly or me against Dad. We'd start on opposite sides of the living room and walk toward each other, and then someone would yell, 'Draw!' Dad would collapse on the carpet and we'd cackle, as Matt Dillon put his smoking gun back in its holster."

(Which reminds me: he always smelled like cigarette smoke when he came home from work, because he treated himself to a single Kent in the car every night. I forgot about that. The smell would fill my nose when I hugged him. That may be why, unlike my wife, I don't mind cigarette smoke at all. In fact I sort of like it.)

"I couldn't get enough of him. On Sunday mornings, when he caught up on sleep for the week, Mom let me wake him, but not until ten o'clock. He would lie on his back with one knee bent, groggy, and I'd slide down his thigh to his belly. Those were the best moments of my childhood.

"A few times, I woke up in the night and found Dad at the kitchen table, bare-chested, having a midnight snack and reading the *New York Post*. (It was a liberal paper then—before Rupert Murdoch.) His preferred snack was rye bread and butter—or else raisin bran that had been in the freezer a while, with little icebergs of milk. He would say, 'Hey, pal, come keep me company,' and I'd sit with him, blinking. All alone with my father while everyone slept: could anything be better? Then he'd walk me back to bed and tuck me in a second time, and kiss my forehead."

(The second pause. The story brought back the kitchen of my childhood: the old refrigerator with rounded doors, and the textured aluminum ice tray with the lever you pulled to crack the ice and free the cubes. It also brought back the time I found him staring grimly at the wall in front of him. I backed away silently, unseen and disturbed. That stare contradicted everything I knew about him. What was he seeing on that blank wall?)

There were murmurs from the pews. Grief distorted my older son's face.

"They had parties with their old friends from Brooklyn once a month. Some of you were there: Snow Weiss and Betty, Bernard and Sarah, Hank, Charlie. There was a bit of dancing, a moderate amount of drinking, and lots of laughter. Dad was the organizer, the one who made the phone calls. This was long before email, before answering machines. It took a lot of time, but he always had energy. By the way, remember those bottles of liquor you brought when the party was at our house? They stayed at the bottom of the broom closet, gathering dust until you came over for another party.

"He loved jokes: hearing them and telling them. At my bar mitzvah, I overheard this punchline: 'I'm telling everybody!' His friends roared. I asked him to tell me, too, and he blushed. Snow promised to tell me the joke when I turned eighteen, but he never did. How about it, Snow? Maybe later today.

"Everyone knows Dad loved to bowl. Until his stroke, he never missed a week. I went to watch him a few times. His right foot did a strange off-balance dance each time he released the ball, but he consistently bowled close to 200, and he had his name etched on his ball, just above the finger holes, which I thought was very cool.

"He also had an unusual amount of emotional intelligence. When he saw my mother sinking into her dark place—which, it's no secret, happened often—he would send one of us to ask her quietly for help with a rip in our pants or a sudden onset of nausea. It didn't always work, but sometimes it was enough to keep her from sinking into her lowest lows.

"His sympathy even extended to Richard Nixon, whom he considered a slimy sneak. When someone asked his opinion about Watergate, Dad said, 'I feel bad for the guy. He only wanted one thing his whole life, he clawed his way up until he got it, and now look at him.'

"They moved to Florida before it was time to retire, because Mom missed her sisters. He found an exterminator he'd known in Queens and arranged to work for him. It couldn't have been easy to take orders from someone else after owning his own business, but he never complained. He said he was happy to leave the headaches behind. If there was something he could do to make Mom happy, he did it, without fail.

"Once they settled in, he was like a religious convert. Every other word out of his mouth was Florida. 'In Florida this,' 'In Florida that.' He took up tennis on the weekends, with tremendous enthusiasm, if not great form. When he ran and hit the ball, he looked like he was swatting a fly with a tomahawk.

"He retired in 1990, and had no trouble filling his days with hobbies and sports. But two months after he stopped working, he came home from tennis and found Mom on the kitchen floor."

Mom's sister Goldie cried out, "Rozzie!"

"It was the worst day of his life. When I finally got down here and walked through the door, we hugged for longer than ever before. That was the second time I saw him cry.

"The first week was rough. It seemed like an unsurvivable blow. What was he going to do with himself, alone and without a job to keep his mind off what he'd lost? After the funeral, when everyone went home, he said to me, 'I'm not sure I can make it.' I wasn't sure, either.

"I stayed with him that week. At one point, he suddenly doubled over. I thought it was about Mom, but no—he had a kidney stone.

"Thanks to his many friends (and I really mean that: thank you), he recovered his spirit. One day Aunt Ruth made an interesting suggestion. She said, 'There are lonely women all around you, Morris. You're a nice guy. Why don't you invite some of them out?'

"If she was scheming to find him a second wife, he didn't seem to notice. So began what Paul and Holly and I called his Take a Widow to Lunch period. He was a rare commodity, if you think about it: healthy, solvent, and pleasant to be around. I talked to him once a week—from the day I left for college until last Saturday—and he would tell me about the women he'd gone to lunch with. He had known most of them for years, and seemed not to suspect that they might be hoping for more than an hour of friendly conversation."

That's how he made it sound, anyway. Now I wonder if he was shopping too. (And I wonder if any of them were sitting in the pews.)

"Then came Charlotte.

"If you've ever seen Charlotte dance, you have an idea of what their life together has been like. Whirling, fast on their feet, they never stopped. It still amazes me that one man could be happy with two women who were so different from each other. But what a relief it was to see him come alive again. They took many trips every year, mostly to Las Vegas, Atlantic City, and assorted Indian-run casinos. She played craps and he watched. (After his childhood, I don't think he could ever take pleasure in watching dollars leave his hand.) They took golf lessons and played together. When they cruised in the Caribbean, she would explore the art galleries in each port and bring back paintings and little sculptures made of driftwood, wire, and bottle-caps. And then there were the Palm Beach shopping sprees."

Her son Joel, a real estate developer, financed those. It was never easy, listening to my father gush over Joel's wealth: his waterfront mansion, his sailboat, his house staff. He didn't realize that his awe at Joel's money made me feel like a failure. I

confess that I smiled inside when I read that Joel had gotten
two years of probation for bribing three of Pompano Beach's
commissioners.

So much had to be left out. The fact that my older brother
and sister had urged him not to marry Charlotte, because it
looked like a terrible mismatch. The fact that, by making her
his second wife, he climbed a few rungs on the social ladder,
because her husband had been a furrier in Manhasset. The fact
that Paul and Holly and I used to call her E.B., for Energizer
Bunny. (I've always liked Charlotte, but she's undeniably hyper-
active.) The fact that she asked him not to set up his clever
innovations in their new home—for example, the toothbrush
holder he made by bending a wire hanger around his fingers—because they didn't go with all that glass, chrome, and
polished stone. The fact that I wished he'd waited more than
a year before remarrying. The fact that their gambling and all
of their other entertainments seemed foolish and wasteful to
me. I know I judged them too harshly. After everything they'd
both lived through, they had a right to indulge themselves. I just
wished they'd chosen better ways to have fun.

"I won't say much about the last few years, because he
wouldn't want us to think of him that way. You can imagine
what a blow it was to realize he'd never bowl or dance or play
golf or tennis again. He didn't complain, though. Instead, he
became a skillful one-handed typist. He spent hours at his
computer, sharing jokes with friends and family, researching
Operation Diadem, the campaign he'd taken part in during the
war, and learning about whatever awoke his curiosity that day:
Vincent Van Gogh, Moshe Dayan, elephant social behavior, the
aqueducts of ancient Rome. He wrote a letter to the *Sun Sentinel*
once, pleading for more civility from people who criticized
President Obama. 'No matter what party you belong to,' he
wrote, 'you have to admit he's smart, dignified, and a devoted
father.' He was proud when they printed his letter, and so was I.

"One of his last remaining pleasures, aside from sneaking
chocolate to his grandchildren, was singing with Joyce, his

health aide. I once came back from driving Charlotte to the eye doctor and heard them singing 'Fly Me to the Moon.' The two accents, Jamaican and Brooklyn, went together very nicely."

The ending I'd composed on the plane didn't seem completely sincere, and I decided at the last minute not to read it. In my written text, I had atoned for portraying him as small and ordinary by exaggerating his stature. *When I compare my generation with his—when I think about everything he survived and the relative comfort of his children's lives—he seems like a giant to me. He overcame poverty, war, and every other challenge life threw at him, and made it look easy.* Instead of reciting this inflated praise, I improvised. "My father was an unusual man. Cheerful, friendly, unassuming. He always bounced back, and he knew how to make other people happy. I've never met anyone like him."

The air at the cemetery was hot and thick. I was glad to have the yarmulke covering the place where my hair is thinnest, but expected my nose to burn. Ellen had brought a little tube of sunscreen, however, and she passed it around. Her eternal preparedness is a running joke in our family.

During the rabbi's prayers, she wove her fingers tightly between mine. Mottled faces surrounded us: Dad's friends, his brother and sister, his neighbors. The turnout lifted me. But I couldn't let go of the fact that my younger son hadn't come. While the rabbi chanted in Hebrew and then courteously translated (*O you who dwell in the shelter of the Most High…*), I grieved over the wrong person. Evan has always been rebellious, defiant; therefore I think about him more than about his brother. Ian, the easy-going entrepreneur, seems to have forgiven whatever mistakes we made along the way. Evan, the prickly one, keeps his resentments close at hand.

A tarp covered Mom's grave. Next to it, the straight walls of the fresh hole waited, along with the mound of earth.

The rabbi took out a clear pouch of amber dirt from Israel. He poured a little into Charlotte's cupped hands, and Paul's, and Holly's, and mine. We gently spilled our portions on the polished coffin, one after another. I was thinking that Dad could probably tell a joke about a burial. I wished I knew it.

ᕦ

Traditionally, only the immediate family gathers at home after the cemetery, for a simple meal prepared by friends—hard-boiled eggs, bagels, and so on. But Charlotte couldn't turn away the relatives who had flown from far-off places, or anyone else. She ordered three giant platters from a deli on Atlantic Avenue: turkey and pastrami, lox, and pineapple and watermelon chunks.

Faces unfamiliar and half-remembered filled the house. Dad would have loved seeing so many people there, talking and laughing.

Someone's grandchild, a toddler, kept trying to topple the glass sculpture on the coffee table. Her mother was engrossed in conversation, so I kept my eye on the little vandal and rescued the blue flame twice. Meanwhile, my son's wife shepherded Olivia and Daniel everywhere, giving each of my aunts and uncles the pleasure of meeting Morris's great-grandchildren. Mother and daughter had matching Julie Andrews haircuts because of a recent lice episode.

Charlotte's son couldn't come back to the house, but both of her daughters were there. I'd only met her granddaughters once, as tiny children at the wedding, but I recognized them from Facebook, where they've been hugging my father for years. Both had smeared their mascara. He explained to me a few years ago that, until they were teenagers, they thought he was their biological grandfather.

Snow Weiss, who's diabetic among other things, looked green. He complained that he spends half his life at funerals, the other half at doctors' offices. His ears have always faced forward, like a chimp's, and his brow, a continuous ridge, reinforces that impression. He was always the swarthiest of my father's friends (the nickname is intentionally ironic), but his hair has gone silver-gray. His eyes still sneak back and forth like he's looking for a way to cheat at something. "Kenny, you got everything right except one thing," he told me. "Your old man had more balls than you think."

Right after the war, he explained, he and Betty went to the Strand in downtown Brooklyn to see a movie. A newsreel about Norman Thomas came on, and some morons in the crowd started heckling the screen, *Shut up, Commie,* and so on. Betty, a sympathizer since childhood, snapped at them. "I want to hear what he's saying." They got into a shouting match, and then the three toughs came down the aisle to teach Snow and his wife about patriotism. He was thinking it would be nuts if he survived three years in the Pacific only to get his skull cracked in a movie theater on Fulton Street. But then, who should stand up but Morris and his brother Sam. "We didn't know they were there. They blocked the aisle—all I saw was Morris reasoning with the shitheads, just long enough for me and Betty to run for the exit. He saved us."

I couldn't picture my father holding off three thugs, but Sam had won a citywide wrestling championship in high school, so it might have happened the way Snow said. Or, he may have massaged the facts a bit, a favor for an old friend.

I wanted it to be true. The possibility that my genial, unassuming father had done something physically courageous made my heart leap.

Dad's old friends, the four who outlived him, have always been as distinct to me as—Snow's name suggested it—the seven dwarfs. Snow is gruff and dark, shady but loyal. Hank Finkel, a retired cabbie, talks a mile a minute and you can't understand half of it. Charlie Feldstein's flat-top makes him look square-headed; when he gets excited or angry, he puts his face too close to the person he's arguing with. Bernard Workman's kindly eyes suggest wise benevolence, but he talks to his friends condescendingly, as if they were idiots.

They were in what Dad used to call the Florida room, where he'd spent so many hours watching cable news. Charlie and Bernard were talking about the Syrian refugees trying to reach Europe on foot, and Hungary putting up a wall to keep them out, and America's feeble response. "We're no better than the countries that refused to take in the Jews." "Americans are fearful, Charlie. They see Muslim and they think terrorist. But I'm more worried about what happens to Israel if Assad falls." "That bastard? He deserves a bomb right on his head." "What comes after him could be worse. The best thing would be if they all keep fighting each other until they can't stand up." "Yeah, that's good for Israel, but what about the ordinary Syrians? They don't deserve this." And Hank: "Hey, if Morris was here, he'd say, Do you have to argue at my funeral?"

Their conversation sent me back to the Thanksgiving when Uncle Sam argued with Evan and my father suffered. Evan had just turned twenty-one, and Sam—whose wife had died that summer—flew up with Dad and Charlotte. Sam urged Evan to take the Birthright trip to Israel, and Evan said, "I'll pass." "No, it's beauty-full," Sam said. "They got more history than anywhere." Evan let loose about Zionism, racism, apartheid, etc., and Sam, confused, asked, "You think we don't need Israel?" Evan said, "Not really. The world has changed."

Charlotte tsked. My father tried to reason with Evan, citing two thousand years of persecution: "There wouldn't have been a Holocaust if we had a place to go." But Evan refused to budge, and my father said, "Kenny, talk to him."

My own attitude toward Israel wobbles between attachment and despair. "It's a problem without a solution," I said. "The Arabs never accepted us, and you can't live under attack for seventy years without your heart hardening."

"They've got to survive!" Sam said. "Hamas keeps shooting rockets over the border. They'd be crazy not to shoot back."

My father said, "Look at us after 9/11. One terrorist attack and we go to war in two countries."

"And look how well that turned out," Evan said.

I thought he was being a jerk, frankly, refusing to see truth in anything they said, making a sport of upsetting them. But I didn't want him to feel I was siding against him. I said, "Isn't it possible that the reason you feel so safe is that we're not a powerless people anymore, dependent on the mercy of our hosts?"

He said, "I don't see that. I feel safe because no one's threatening me."

He went further—so far that he claimed Israel's behavior had provoked much of the world's recent anti-Jewish feeling—until Sam, the most loving of my uncles, blurted out, "Traitor!" My father pleaded with his brother. "Sam..." He looked ill.

In deference to his brother, Sam clammed up. He was sweating and too upset to make peace. Charlotte said, "He's just a kid. He'll learn." Evan opened his mouth, but Ellen pointed the Finger of Silence at him.

I searched for words that would bridge the gulf between my father's generation and my son's, and came up with nothing.

Ian said, "It's weird that we're so worked up about this when none of us ever goes to synagogue." He was trying to lighten the mood, but it didn't work.

Ellen and Charlotte took up some inoffensive subject after that. My father stared into the purple stain of cranberry sauce on his plate. I've never seen him so defeated.

The memory of that unhappy face made me wince. Friends and neighbors filled the room with chattering life, but the owner of the house was gone. I rested my hand on the top of the recliner where he'd spent most of his waking hours for the past six years. The leather was cold.

Charlotte's brother had brought his daughter, a very thin philosophy professor. I'd met Genevieve once before, at Dad's wedding, and found her flirtatious, exciting, and dauntingly smart. (Ellen had stayed home with Ian and Evan, both of whom had strep throat.) We danced, fast then slow—I'd had three drinks, which is a lot for me—and even though she had thin lips and pock-marked cheeks, I found her smile thrilling. Her fingers were small as a child's. We were both damp with sweat, but I pulled her against me. Then I became aware of the eyes on us, including my father's. We finished the dance; I thanked her, she bowed, and I returned to my table.

She wore a sleeveless navy-blue dress today. Once again, all these years later, she wore no rings.

We couldn't flirt under the circumstances, but that made talking more comfortable. She asked how I was doing. "Fair to good," I said, and told her she looked great. She said my beard was an excellent choice. I asked if she was still teaching, and she said, "Unfortunately."

"Remind me: what kind of philosophy do you teach?"

"Aesthetics. But I should have stuck with dance. Too much mind, not enough body."

The acne scars were still there, but her gray eyes seemed so alive, so full of nimble thoughts, so attentive. I would have been happy to spend the rest of the day with her.

She said she'd loved the eulogy. I told her I'd left a lot out. "Like what?" she asked. I didn't want to criticize my father, here of all places, but I admitted that, when I hear men say things like, *I admire my dad more than anyone I've ever met*, it makes me shake my head. "You think it's baloney?"

"No, I envy them. Some fathers really are heroic. I wanted mine to be like that." (And I wanted to be like that myself, I thought. I didn't manage it, though.)

"Your father really was a great guy. He seemed nice through and through."

"You're right, he was."

But she said she understood. "My mother is a cold fish. No amount of therapy will stop me from wishing I had someone else's."

My sister interrupted us. She wanted me to set up the coffee urn. "I'll talk to you again later," I said, and Genevieve replied, "Looking forward to it."

We never did finish that conversation. When she came to say goodbye, I apologized for that. "Are you kidding?" she said. We shook hands. "Till next time," I said. "Adios, amigo," she replied.

A sliding door in the Florida room looks out on the coarse grass behind the house. I leaned against it and eavesdropped. "We took our grandchildren to see snow. They hadn't been out of the state before." "They never saw a *rock*. There are no rocks in Florida." "Is that really true?"

A woman with peach-blonde hair like Charlotte's elbowed her husband and glanced at me guiltily. Their chatter hadn't offended me, though. The buzz of normal life was soothing.

Two teenagers sat on the long white couch in the living room, where no one ever sits. The boy was blowing into his iPhone and making fluty sounds. The girl took a video of him and happily sent it off somewhere. She was pretty but wore so much foundation that her skin looked like a leg in pantyhose. The boy was good-looking, too, though his hair stood up ridiculously, like Tintin's.

They reminded me a little of my parents in old photos, fooling around before the war. That black-and-white world has always looked so simple and innocent to me—like Eden in Brooklyn. I know there was more to their lives than dancing on tarpaper roofs and posing like a muscle man on the beach, but think of everything that hadn't happened yet: Pearl Harbor, Hitler, Hiroshima—the Cold War, Mao—JFK's assassination, Vietnam—Watergate, AIDS, 9/11. Other than poverty, what complicated their happiness back in the summer of 1941? Nothing I know of.

My brother's grandson, whose father is Mexican, had brought some Squigz to entertain himself. He was helping Daniel, my grandson, build a rocket with the colorful rubbery pawns, sticking them together under the friendly supervision of a teenage Asian girl. (I have no idea who she was.) The three of them made a Norman Rockwell picture. I wished I could show Dad.

Late in the afternoon, my brother and sister and I occupied the long white couch. All three of us still wore our little black ribbons, which the rabbi's brawny assistant had slit on one side with a razor. Behind us, the front window looked out on a flat-topped ficus and a straight-edged lawn. Not a single weed dared peek between the creamy paving stones of the driveway.

I asked if they had ever felt as if Dad might be an imposter, pretending everything was just fine, refusing to complain even though he had reason to.

Paul dismissed that. He's been preoccupied with financial worries since he opened his music store forty years ago, and has never troubled himself over our father's psyche. "If that's what he was doing, he was right. I complain every day and it doesn't help."

Holly saw my point, but she also saw beyond it. "He had so much to get through, Kenny. That was the only way he knew how."

We hadn't talked this way in years. To keep it going, I asked if they'd ever seen Dad depressed when we were little. But Charlotte joined us on the couch, and then the guests started coming over to take their leave, and that was that. Clasping her hands, one after another, they said things like, "He was a wonderful man" and "I'll call you."

All day, Charlotte had hosted with her usual energy, only slightly dimmed. It was obvious that she had taken some kind of pill to get through this—which was just like her. Nothing can slow her down or drag her under. In that way, she's the exact opposite of Mom, who lived half her life submerged.

Although Charlotte stocked their house with colorful folk art from Jamaica, Puerto Rico, Trinidad, and the Bahamas, the rooms have always felt chilly to me. None of it has much to do with my father. (One exception: his photo of a yellow tree and reddish Vermont hills, framed in the kitchen.)

They used to be fanatics when it came to cleaning. My sons used to tease my father about the compulsive way he wiped down the kitchen counter after every meal and snack. But now the bathroom exhaust fan is clogged with dust, and cobwebs cross the ceiling corners in every room. Neither of them can see it.

I was in the guest room, reading the dates on the spines of Dad's photo albums, when Ian came to say goodbye. Sunny held Olivia and Daniel by the hand. "Sorry we can't stay longer," he said. "I'm engineering a demo in the morning, and I promised the band I'd do it myself."

"I'm grateful that you came. And thanks for bringing the family."

He heard the implication. "Evan would've come if he could. His life is crazier than mine."

Sunny sent the kids to me for hugs. Usually I bring them something—a magnifying glass, a yo-yo, a gyroscope (my losing battle against the iPad)—but that hadn't happened today. I told Olivia I wished I could have read a book with her, and she, with her tiny teeth, said, "That's okay, Grandpa, you had a lot to do."

Daniel smelled like peanut butter and shampoo. "I'm always happy to see you, little man," I said.

He sang, "Happy to see you"—a snatch of "Cabaret," I think.

My son hugged me. "You gonna be okay, Dad?"

"I'm fine."

"You got more emotional up there than I think I ever saw you."

"It caught me by surprise. I thought I had it under control."

"That's insane. How could you not choke up? You only get one father."

I kissed his cheek, which is fleshier than mine, and thanked the universe that our long-ago battles over his nightly pot-smoking didn't alienate him forever.

After we packed away the leftovers and folded the rental chairs, we had a pizza delivered. (Terrible, even by Florida standards.) Then Charlotte went to the mall with her daughter and granddaughter, who needed a new charging cable for her phone. I tried to write some notes for work, couldn't focus, and took a walk with Ellen instead.

It was dusk by then: a golden horizon, inky blue above. A few stars had already appeared. We had the streets to ourselves.

Where every other yard had a palm tree, the next-door neighbor had planted a pair of flowerbeds. "They look like graves," my father said when I visited the first time. But that was many years ago. The luminous flowers now seemed more alive than anything else on the street.

The development had been brand-new then. The foundation plantings were little green pom-poms, and you could smell the road tar. Now his street has long sealed cracks like surgical scars, and the bushes have to be trimmed so they don't block the windows.

I used to hate the damp heat, the flat terrain, the dull routines of retirement. Tonight the landscape almost appealed to me.

In a lit window, a seated man's head glided across his living room. In rushed the memory of Joyce transferring Dad from the bed to the wheelchair. First she sat him up on the edge of the bed; then she put her arms around him, gripped the gait belt, and counted, "One, two, tree," before lifting him like a sack and pivoting to deposit him in the chair.

He didn't like my seeing that.

Ellen gave me space and quiet. Hearing a squeak, she asked gently, "Are you all right?"

"More or less."

"Go on."

"He had such a hard time the last few years."

She took my arm. It was good to walk together. Sometimes she does exactly the right thing.

I was brushing my teeth, gazing at the painted wooden rooster and the wire Romeo and Juliet on the glass shelf, when Charlotte stopped in the doorway. With her makeup scrubbed away, she seemed smaller, exposed. The raised mole between her eyebrows looked like a dark bindi dot.

"I found some things of your father's. They're in the kitchen."

She spoke tersely, severely. That worried me. I hoped for bowling trophies, and feared a stash of pornography.

The cardboard box on the kitchen table said *Spiratone* on the side. I hadn't seen that script-like logo in many decades. Paper tape girdled the box; clear packing tape had been added later.

"I was putting his clothes in a bag for Goodwill yesterday and I found this up on the shelf."

We sat with the box between us. My family's old address in Queens was handwritten on the mailing label.

The holes in her earlobes, where her heavy earrings usually hung, were lines, not dots. Her face shone with cold cream; the pores on her nose were clogged with it. For as long as I've known her, Charlotte has cleaned her face with Noxzema every night. Twenty years from now, when she's gone, that smell of camphor, menthol, and eucalyptus will live on in my nostrils.

She waited for me to explore the contents of the box. She didn't look happy.

I found a bulging manila envelope, a Daffodil Farm bread bag filled with tarnished coins, a sealed white envelope with no address, a small gray cube that had once held a Timex watch, a folder of comic strip-style drawings, a drawstring bag with something hard and heavy inside, a couple greeting cards, and two letters addressed to my father, one at Muller's, one in Queens.

"You should look at this first."

She tapped the manila envelope, which held a sheaf of old newspaper articles. Each had been clipped neatly along the hairline separating columns. Some still had the dates on top. They were all from 1954.

The first article included a narrow photo of Adam Clayton Powell Jr., a dapper Black congressman whose name I remembered from childhood. *ASSAILANT CAPTURED,* said the headline. The subhead read, *Hidden by Friend in Queens Apt.* Why my father had saved this article from three months before I was born, I couldn't guess—until I noticed our name halfway down the page. *Police officers found Rosario hiding in Weintraub's Rego Park apartment.* According to the article, a man named German Rosario had tried to assassinate the congressman, but his shots had missed their target. My father's full name appeared one paragraph up: *Arrested along with Rosario was Morris Weintraub, a suspected accomplice.*

"What's this about?" I asked.

"When I opened the envelope, that was the first I heard of it. I don't know how he could have kept it secret all these years."

"It must have been a mistake. He never mentioned it?"

"Never. You'd think in twenty-four years, a man would tell his wife something like that."

She sounded distressed, close to tears. She looked at me like a hurt child.

"There has to be an explanation. This doesn't make sense."

"Why didn't he trust that I would understand?"

"We should ask my aunts and uncles. They must know what happened."

She agreed. Then she said she needed to go to bed.

I read the clippings alone. According to the first article, Rosario, a Puerto Rican from the Bronx, had fired a pistol at Congressman Powell as he entered his district office in Harlem on March 3, 1954—two days after Puerto Rican nationalists fired from the gallery of the Capitol in Washington, wounding five representatives. The police believed that Rosario might belong to the same organization. Three shots had been fired; the bullets hit a glass door, a bystander's hat, and a brick wall. Police had arrested Rosario and my father, but not my pregnant mother, because the officers determined that she had been an unwilling accessory. The fact that she had two small children in her care may have influenced their decision.

Skimming the articles, I learned that the judge sentenced him to three years.

I couldn't imagine my father harboring a would-be assassin, and still can't. The idea of him belonging to a radical Puerto Rican political organization is so absurd, it reminds me of one of his jokes: *A guy I know signed up to be a terrorist, but he's so dumb, when they told him to blow up a car, he burned his mouth on the tailpipe.*

I find it hard to believe that he spent three years in prison. If that really happened, wouldn't it have left a shadow?

Hoping for some sort of clue that would explain everything, I opened the white envelope. Inside was the photo of him with Silvia, in Rome.

There's so much I wish I could ask him.

2

The clippings are ochre, and brittle. I'm handling them as carefully as I can, but unfolding the paper has opened a slit where the first article was creased.

Neither Rosario nor Weintraub attempted to flee, according to police spokesman Vincent Dikeman. He described Rosario as "cooperative and submissive."

It remains to be seen whether or not the incident was the second in a wave of attempted assassinations. "I guess we'll know pretty soon," Lt. Dikeman commented.

But why Adam Clayton Powell?

I remember him as a handsome man in a suit, with a mustache like Duke Ellington's. Nothing I can find links him to the Puerto Rican independence movement—except, possibly, the fact that his third wife was Puerto Rican. But he didn't marry her until six years later.

The two men served in Italy together during the War, in I Company, 339th Infantry. When questioned by investigators, both Rosario and Weintraub denied wrongdoing. Rosario claims this is a case of mistaken identity. Weintraub said he is "a hundred percent sure" his friend is innocent.

But the resemblance between Rosario and the police sketch is striking, from the mustache to the scar on the side of the neck.

Rosario insists he was out walking on his lunch hour at the time of the shooting, but has not produced a witness. He works as a custodian at P.S. 71 in the Pelham Bay section of the Bronx.

Morris Weintraub, the Rego Park man who is charged with sheltering the accused assailant of Rep. Adam Clayton Powell Jr., testified in state court on Thursday that he hadn't seen or spoken to Rosario since 1945. "When

I saw the police sketch in the paper, I got worried," he said. He telephoned Rosario but no one answered. He claims he went to help Rosario "on impulse" and found him in a panic.

Weintraub admits that he offered to hide Rosario in his Queens apartment, "just until we could get him a lawyer and maybe find the old woman who saw him walking." (Rosario claims he often took long walks on his lunch hour, to look out at Eastchester Bay from the end of Lucerne Street.)

As they entered Weintraub's apartment building on Sixty-Third Drive, however, a neighbor recognized Rosario from the police sketch and called the police.

On Monday in state court, Morris Weintraub of Queens pleaded guilty to one count of hindering prosecution. He had initially pleaded not guilty.

He faces a penalty of up to three years in prison. Judge Harold Merksamer will determine his sentence at a future hearing.

What if Rosario was innocent, though? Would they still put the guy who helped him in prison?

The Queens man who pleaded guilty to harboring Rep. Adam Clayton Powell Jr.'s accused assailant was sentenced today to three years in prison, the maximum allowable penalty.

In a statement to the court, Morris Weintraub asked for mercy, explaining that his friend feared he would be wrongly convicted if arrested. He said he only wanted to give Rosario a chance to prove his innocence.

Judge Merksamer lectured Weintraub from the bench. "First you put your friendship with this man above the safety of the public. Now you insult the criminal justice system. I will not go easy on you. I intend to discourage others from following your example."

When the judge pronounced sentence, Weintraub's wife groaned audibly. She was helped out of the courtroom by the defendant's brother.

All right. This I can understand. He wasn't a conspirator, just a friend, helping out an old army buddy.

He found Rosario in a panic. The clippings don't tell what happened to Rosario at trial. I wonder if he lied to Dad about his innocence—if he panicked because he knew there was no way to escape punishment.

And Mom: trivial problems made her frantic. I can't imagine how she coped with this.

The maximum allowable penalty. What a bastard. I hope they caught him taking a bribe, or stalking his ex-mistress. I hope he got the maximum allowable penalty himself.

Three objects stand on the narrow shelf above this kitchen table: a carved wooden shore bird, sanded smooth, on legs thinner than straws; a bottle painted turquoise and ultramarine; and a roughly carved wooden horse, smaller than my hand. On the wall in front of me is a small painting of five boys fishing at dusk, in glowing T-shirts of different rainbow colors, their skin nearly black. It's easy to picture Charlotte in her floppy sun hat, browsing in one island art gallery after another while Dad tagged along, never knowing what would appeal to her or why.

The chairs are white bamboo. The wallpaper is sand-colored linen. The polished granite table matches the countertop. I wonder if he sometimes felt like a guest here.

The two letters are still in their pink envelopes. One is postmarked 1945, the other 1956. Both letters are in Spanish, and printed in capital letters. The *M*s look like little suspension bridges, each with a wide catenary connecting the towers; the *E*s look like backward 3s. At the bottom of both letters is the name Nydia Rosario. The address on the back of both envelopes is 601 West 148th street, New York, New York.

I'll ask Myriam to translate when I get back to the office. I wonder who Dad asked.

"What's going on? You went to brush your teeth and never came back."

Ellen is squinting. She must have fallen asleep.

Her hair has frizzed out wider than usual at the bottom. It's iron-gray and silver, with just a little black remaining in the curls behind her neck. I'd like to tell her everything—but she's an erratic sleeper. Say the wrong thing and she's up till dawn.

"What's all this?"

"Some mementos of my father's. Charlotte thought I'd like to see them."

"You should come to bed. You can look at them in the morning."

"I just want to see what's here. I'll be in soon."

She leaves, frowning. This once, she doesn't complain that I'll wake her when I come in.

The first time we visited together, he watched her at the pool and said, "Her figure is like Mommy's." He meant when they were young; my mother never looked like that (slim on top, wider at the hips) during my lifetime. I had told Ellen that he loved jokes, and she impressed him with one she'd heard from her old roommate, a Swedish exchange student. Apparently Fälldin, the prime minister, was considered a dolt by some, and he inspired a whole genre of jokes. One day he gets into a cab and the driver says, "Have you heard the latest Fälldin joke?" The prime minister tells the driver indignantly, "*I'm* Fälldin," and the driver says, "Okay, I'll tell it slowly." Dad had her write the name longhand—this was before everyone had a computer—and I heard him tell the joke to his friends, crediting "Kenny's new girlfriend, who's beautiful, by the way." We were all happier once Ellen arrived on the scene.

Let's see what's in the Timex box.

Four bullets, the shafts black, the rounded tips copper. A strange ring with a blue oval stone mounted on a silver kite, like something Wonder Woman might wear. A military patch, two pale green bars on a field of darker green, with a rusty stain.

The canvas drawstring bag holds a black pistol with a narrow cylindrical barrel and a round trigger guard. I know nothing about guns, but this looks like the kind German officers would point at the hero in old movies.

I doubt I'll ever know how he ended up with these things.

There's more.

A birthday card from Aunt Ruth, addressed to him in Johnson City. *You should think about moving back here. We miss you.*

A Christmas card signed *German & Marquita, Oscar & Elsie.* No note, just the names.

A folder of cartoon drawings in pencil. One character has Dagwood-style hair, four horizontal lines on each side of his head. Another has a big muscular chest like Li'l Abner, and wears an old-timey tank-top bathing suit.

The coins are gray like old nickels, with some blackening around the edges. They seem to be replicas of ancient coins, with Roman numerals on the front.

Aha. On the back, each coin illustrates a different sexual position. Men with laurel wreaths, grinning. A woman with thin arms, stoically handling an upright little rocket.

He was eighteen when he left, twenty when he came home. A kid—possibly a virgin. The coins must have seemed like hot stuff in 1945. Or maybe he thought they were funny. I wonder.

In the photo with Silvia, his uniform shirt has long sleeves, though it's July in Rome. There are two chevrons on his shoulder patch, with a *T* nestled underneath. Her dress is white, printed with tiny flowers, and just covers her knees. It looks lightweight, the kind of fabric a soft breeze could lift. There's a low concrete wall behind them, its outer skin peeling away in patches. They seem to be on a rooftop. Nothing in the background identifies the location. Silvia's hair is short, black, curly. She's squinting in the sun—not beautiful, but sexy in a rough way.

I don't think she was just a grateful Italian citizen, posing with a friendly American liberator. She's leaning too insistently against him, as if declaring ownership. Then there's the fact that he kept the envelope sealed.

If the photo had been taken in a small town, I could have sent a copy to the local newspaper and asked if anyone recognized this woman. That won't work in Rome.

Did he write to her? One of the nuns from Muller's could have translated his letter into Italian. He'd have had a hard time pouring his heart out with a nun listening in, though.

If my father defied the law to save an innocent friend from prison, then he was loyal and brave, and I should treasure the news. But the story has me unsettled. I've dismissed him as a meek little man for the last fifty years. The injustice of that...

3

My brother had no memory of police coming to the apartment. "What are you talking about?" He was already at his store. A trombone played in the background.

He would have been six at the time. You'd think a person would remember something like that—unless the cops sent the kids off to play before they put the cuffs on.

He didn't want to let me off the phone. "If you know something, tell me."

I said I was still trying to figure it out, and promised to explain soon.

I filled Ellen in while she was getting dressed. She stopped and stared at me in her bra and capris. I showed her the articles; she skimmed the first one, then the second.

"Holy shit. You never knew?"

"Not until last night."

She looked over the rest of the articles. A hardness came over her face.

"Are you angry at my father for not telling us?"

"No, I want to kill the judge."

That was satisfying to hear. "It's possible he was pardoned. Maybe they caught the real shooter. Maybe he never went to prison."

She shook her head: a small, unreadable gesture.

I told her I wanted to get my aunts and uncles together and ask questions. Our flight was at three-thirty; it was already nine. "Better start dialing," she said.

I had their information at home, but I've never entered it in my phone. Charlotte, still in her long nightgown, brought my father's address book to the kitchen table. She had already put on her makeup; the mole was only faintly visible now. She'd set out a few boxes of cereal for us, along with two bowls, two glasses, and a green jar of Folgers instant decaf, the only coffee they keep in the house. She said less than on any other morning I've spent in Florida.

"Would you like to come to lunch with us?" I asked.

"No, it's too much. You can tell me what you find out."

The address book had a padded cover that simulated dark wood. The spine had been repaired with black electrical tape. He'd crossed out and replaced many of the addresses, some more than once. His handwriting made me smile: slanting left, slanting right, no two loops the same. Under *W*, Paul and Judy came first, then Holly (even though she changed her name to McCafferty; Chris was crossed out), then Kenny and Ellen. After his three children came his brother Sam.

When I told Aunt Ruth that I'd read a stack of articles about my father's arrest and trial, she didn't reply. I worried for a moment that she would scold me for digging up something my father wanted to stay buried.

"I knew you'd find out someday. I thought it would happen while he was alive."

I said I hoped that all of them—her, Irv, Sam, Trudy, Goldie, and Julius—would come to lunch and tell me what they knew. She recommended a place called Mr. Chen's.

Sam and Goldie both agreed to come. Trudy, Mom's younger sister—the black sheep—said she would like to but she had an appointment at the beauty parlor and she wouldn't be able to get another slot for a week.

Charlotte watched somberly from the front door as we loaded our suitcases into the trunk of the rental car. She had given me an old vinyl carry-on bag that said, *Maupintour USA*. Inside were my father's secrets, except for the gun and bullets, which would never get through security.

I had a hard time finding words. Ellen said, "It's good that you have your kids nearby."

"Mm-hm. But they have lives of their own."

Ellen hugged her first, then I did. Her shoulders surprised

me: they were so delicate. "Thank you for taking care of him all these years."

"He made me happy every day." She fought hard not to cry. I loved her more at that moment than I ever have before.

"I'll call you soon," I said, and cringed at the sound of my own rote words.

We exchanged small waves through the windshield as I backed out. She went inside before we pulled away.

Mr. Chen's could have been a Chinese restaurant anywhere in the United States—big fish tank, framed calligraphy—except that every seated man had white hair, and so did half the women. The others had opted for colors in the narrow range between peach and strawberry blonde.

My aunts and uncles have always meant Childhood to me. The ones who are left are in their nineties now and barely hanging on.

Although she has lost a few inches, Aunt Ruth—oldest and tallest of Dad's siblings—still carries herself regally. She wore an ankle-length dress printed with red and blue roses and seemed pale even in makeup. Her hair has always been short, with swirls like a frosted cake, but today you could see her scalp through it. Uncle Irv, her husband, wore black compression socks up to his knees, and walked with a four-footed cane. A tough engineer who used to supervise construction workers, he cursed constantly; now his shoulders slump far forward, and he has purple bruises up and down his arms. He dressed neatly for the occasion, though. His khaki shorts had a straight crease, and his lemony polo shirt showed not a wrinkle. "Charlotte couldn't take us two days in a row, huh?" he said.

So many infirmities have overtaken them. Aunt Goldie, in assisted living, uses a walker. Her fingers are fat and crooked, but she still wears gaudy rings on four of them. Her husband, Uncle Julius, used to remind me of the Mole Men in that old *Superman* episode because of his high bald dome. The gray button of his medical alert necklace was the diameter of a tennis ball. Uncle Sam, who used to look like a bodybuilder in swimming trunks, seemed small and frail in his wheelchair. He'd had a basal cell carcinoma removed from his nose a few days before, and some blood had seeped through the dressing. His health aide (Haitian, I think) had to cut his meat for him, because a stroke left him unable to use his right hand and leg. Just like Dad.

All of these people had grown up in Brooklyn and then spread out to raise their families. They converged on Florida in retirement, and now live within a few miles of each other. Much more than my generation, these siblings are like limbs of the same organism; instinctively, they sought each other in order to form a whole again.

I had limited time and specific questions to ask, but I found myself making cheerful small talk as they studied their menus. "I remember all of your houses so clearly," I said, and ticked off the details: the chickadees at the birdfeeder on Ruth's patio, the ping pong table and mounted deer's head in Sam's basement, the somber brown portrait of Mom's grandparents in Goldie's musty apartment, which terrified me. (My great-grandfather's skullcap rose from his head like a short black chef's hat.)

Flashes of memory:

Ruth benignly watching the little cousins chase each other around her yard. Craig's bar mitzvah at Leonard's—the giant crystal chandelier, and relatives of all ages doing the Alley Cat. Sam and Phoebe serving us corn on the cob on paper plates after we spent the afternoon splashing in their pool with cousin Dougie (making huge waves with air mattresses, soaking the grass in a ring around the pool), and how Dad would stand the corn on end and cut it off the cob for me in slices that looked like pieces of honeycomb. Sam, retired, showing Ellen and me the magic tricks he performed in nursing homes: "The chances of matching up all three colors are very nil." Irv teasing me when I was eleven, "You got a girlfriend yet?" I froze and reddened, because I had a cataclysmic crush on Lori F. (Irv's one of my favorite people, but back then he scared me.)

Waiters delivered two steel teapots and eight glasses of water. My aunts and uncles ordered the old-fashioned dishes, the ones without chili peppers next to their names, the same ones my parents used to order when we went to Wayne Wong. Chicken lo mein, sweet and sour pork, beef egg foo young, shrimp with lobster sauce. Goldie asked for a mai tai.

The oldest waiter, dark and quick, had intelligent eyes and commanded the younger men impatiently. I wondered what sort of life he'd led before he came here. To my aunts and uncles, however, he was invisible.

I asked Sam whether he and Dad had really rescued Snow Weiss in a movie theater. He grinned lopsidedly. "I guess we did," he said, and told a different version of the story. My father had tried to calm the jerks down; they cursed him; Sam told them to watch their language; they tried to push the brothers out of the way, and one guy shoved Dad so hard, he fell and cut his chin on a chair arm. Sam slugged the guy, so the other two came after him. But some vets in the audience jumped up to help, because Dad had on his Eisenhower jacket. "That jacket is what saved us," Sam said. That, and the ushers who told them all to get back in their seats or they'd be thrown out of the theater.

Sam offered to tell more "antidotes," and shared one that I might have included in the eulogy if I'd ever heard it before. My father used to go with a pretty Irish girl named Claire before he met Mom, but Grandpa told him never to see her again. He didn't listen, and Grandpa saw them out the window holding hands. When Dad walked in, Grandpa slapped him. That was the end of Claire.

The soup arrived, and the reviews followed. "This broth is just water and salt." "Mine is too bland, I can't taste anything." "Mine is okay. Not great." "You'd think these people ate at the Four Seasons every day."

Ellen couldn't reach my watch, so she tapped her own, *tick-tick-tick*.

I thanked them for agreeing to come. "You know what I want to ask you about. My father obviously wanted to keep it secret, but the secret's out. I'd like to hear what really happened."

The quiet surprised me. For the first time, we could hear voices from other tables.

Sam said softly, "We promised him we'd never mention it."

"He was ashamed," Ruth said. "He didn't want you to know. And we respected his wishes."

Though Irv was at the other end of the table, he looked me straight in the eye. "He thought it might hurt you—all three of you. He was afraid it would mess you up."

Goldie had nothing to say: a first. Uncle Julius, who hasn't spoken more than five words in my presence in my entire lifetime, stared slightly down, like an arcade fortune-teller before you put the coin in.

"Here's a specific question. The articles said he believed the other guy was innocent. Is that right?"

"Absolutely," Ruth said. "I listened to him in court. Morris couldn't lie."

Goldie sneered. "Everyone can lie."

Irv cast his eyes at the ceiling: *I still have to listen to her shit.* Julius blew on a spoonful of soup.

"What about all of you?" I asked them. "Do *you* think Rosario was innocent?"

Ruth, Irv, and Sam agreed that Morris was no fool. He'd known the guy well. If he swore there was no way he would have tried to shoot a congressman, that was good enough for them. Goldie kept her doubts to herself.

I knew so little. I didn't even know what prison my father had gone to.

"He was at Oneida, near Utica," Sam said. "I visited once a month."

"We all did. We took turns," Ruth said.

"We brought him things he asked for," Irv said. "Oranges, Oreos. Remember that art book? I called ten bookstores—nobody had it but Sam Flax."

"My father asked for an art book?"

"It showed you how to draw comics," Ruth said. "He had a talent for it. He thought he might be able to turn it into a career."

"*Draw and Laugh*, it was called," Irv said. "Or *Laugh and Draw*."

That explained the folder of drawings—and the cartoon of himself with a tank of insecticide that he painted on the window of their little storefront on Springfield Boulevard. In it, he had a mustache, a Mets cap, and a pot belly. Three cockroaches fled in terror.

I asked why he never pursued it.

"He had to support a family," Sam said. "He didn't know how to break in."

That stung. He might have found a way to earn a living with his talent, but he never got the chance because of us.

"How did he seem when you visited?"

Sam shrugged. "Like you said yesterday, he didn't complain."

Irv said, "He made a couple friends. One was a counterfeiter. I forget what the other one did. They weren't tough guys, but they'd all been in the service. They looked out for each other."

"Were there any fights, that you know of?"

"He never mentioned it," Irv said. "But you can't tell with Morris, he's good at covering up."

Now that we had started, they seemed eager to hand off as much information as they could. Sam said, "He always told me, 'I'm fine.' He wouldn't go into details. He just wanted to hear about what was going on outside."

"That's understandable," Ruth said. "We were his window to the world."

She looked down, away from me. I asked, "What is it?" and she shook her head. "He was very upset that he couldn't be there when you were born. He said his kids wouldn't remember him when he came home."

At rest, Goldie's lips form a bitter curl. The curl sharpened now. "He should have thought about that before he ruined Rozzie's life."

"He didn't ruin her life," Ruth said quietly.

"She didn't tell you, she told me. She wasn't strong and he left her alone with three babies. It's a miracle she survived."

Irv said, "Hey!" and nodded toward me. "Kenny just lost his father."

I wanted to ask *how* my mother had survived. The only job she'd ever held, as far as I knew, was keeping the books for their business.

Goldie answered my question before I could ask it. "We had to babysit so she could work. She got a job in the office at Queens General Hospital. Her boss was a bitch, she wouldn't even let her go to the bathroom. Mrs. Lenihan. She made Rozzie's life hell."

Venting this ancient hatred, Goldie looked a little like Gloria Swanson in *Sunset Boulevard.* She had wanted to be an actress when she was young, and that made sense. Her drama belonged on a stage.

She wasn't done. "He cared more about a Puerto Rican criminal than his own family."

Sam reached across himself to put his good hand on my arm. "You know that's bull, Kenny. He just wanted to do what was right."

"How was that right? Hiding a crazy killer from the cops?"

"We heard you the first time," Irv said.

Julius stared past my shoulder, past the cashier, out the front door.

Goldie's ranting didn't upset me. Her face is my mother's, almost—just as Ruth's is my father's. Now that both of my parents are gone, these traces of them are precious.

I asked what they knew about Rosario. Sam said, "He was a shrimp who got pushed around a lot when they were overseas. That's what Morris told me. He felt bad for him."

"I'll tell you the saddest part," Ruth said. "He truly believed the judge would sympathize if he just explained. He thought any decent person would do what he did."

"What a son of a bitch that judge was," Irv said. "He had glasses like Woodrow Wilson. He looked like he hadn't gotten laid in fifty years."

"Lovely," Ruth said.

"And I hate to say it, but Morris could have got off with a lot less time if he'd kept his mouth shut."

Ruth defended her younger brother. "He wanted to tell his side of the story. He knew he didn't deserve prison."

Irv addressed me, ignoring his wife. "The old bastard wanted to see remorse. Morris didn't get the message."

"I thought he was just anti-Semitic," Sam said, rhyming the word with *athletic.*

"You're all making excuses," Goldie said. "He wrecked their lives for nothing. That's what he accomplished—nothing."

Ruth responded calmly. She had heard this before. "He didn't wreck their lives. They raised three wonderful children. They ran a successful business. They had plenty of friends."

"*And* he lost his job. *And* they had to move to that shithole in the middle of nowhere. Every time I called, she cried on the phone."

No one argued. I assumed she had won that point.

Ellen said, "To be fair, Roz tended toward depression. In the years I knew her, at least."

"Exactly," Irv said.

Ruth's features contracted in pained sympathy. "Kenny, you know I loved your mother dearly. She was a kind, sweet person. But Ellen is right. There was always a dark cloud over her, even before your father went to prison."

"It didn't come from nowhere," Goldie said. "She had her reasons."

"I'm not criticizing her. I think it was a matter of brain chemistry. Today, they would treat it. Your father was that way too." Ruth turned from Goldie back to me. "You know your grandfather died in a mental hospital, don't you?"

Goldie's lipstick was deep red, too deep for a woman of her age and pallor, but her cheeks began to catch up. "You don't know anything about it!"

Faces at other tables turned our way. Uncle Sam's aide sipped her soup daintily, keeping her eyes down.

"It wasn't a happy marriage," Goldie said. "She almost left him. I thought she should have."

Everyone in the family knows that you can't win an argument with Goldie. Nevertheless, Ruth refused to let that stand.

"It wasn't easy for either of them. Especially after he got out of prison. Roz had a hard time adjusting. But that doesn't mean they were always unhappy. I'm sure you can remember better times, Kenny."

"I do. A few."

Two waiters came to collect our bowls. Goldie waited for them to leave—but Irv jumped in ahead of her. "I want to get back to Kenny's questions, while we're still here to answer them. Go ahead, shoot."

An awkward lead-in, but okay.

"What happened to German Rosario?" I asked. "I assume he went to prison too."

"He pronounced it *Herman*," Irv said. "Yeah, they convicted him."

None of them had followed the story after that. They didn't know how many years he served, or what happened to him afterwards.

"I can understand Dad keeping all this secret when we were little. But to *never* tell us…"

"After so many years, they didn't want to dredge it up again," Ruth said. "That's what I think."

Irv wagged his fork. "Say you're him. If you tell your kids, they might look at you different—as an ex-con. Would you take the chance?"

"As far as I'm concerned," Ruth said, "what Morris did was courageous. It was like running into a burning building."

Courageous. The word sent me back to a moment I haven't thought of in years. As the waiters served our entrees, I saw myself standing on the brick steps outside our kitchen door in Bellerose. Dad—bare-chested, except for all that hair—was pushing the old reel mower around the yard. It was after dinner and I'd just told him I wanted to skip school the next day and go to a demonstration in the city. Kent State had happened a few days before. It was important, I said. We had to show the government that soldiers couldn't shoot protesters, and that we weren't afraid.

He didn't want me to go. "The world is falling to pieces, anything could happen."

I reminded him that this was New York, not Ohio. No one was going to shoot a bunch of students in the middle of Manhattan.

He said there were people here who hated hippies and protesters too.

"It's up to us to stand up and say no," I said. (The memory of my self-righteousness is hard to bear.) "If we stay home, then the bad guys win."

What it was really about was the need to act selflessly for a good cause. My father had gone to Europe to fight Hitler. He'd gotten shot, and saved the world. What had I ever done?

He spoke almost apologetically. "These things get out of hand. They arrest people. I don't want you going to jail."

The war had happened many years before. All I saw in front of me was a chubby middle-aged man clattering around his yard, trimming his little patch of grass. I had no idea.

"Sometimes you have to take a risk," I declared. "Sometimes you have to be brave."

He pushed the mower carefully around the apple tree he'd planted when we moved in. I had accused him of being a coward, even though it was me he was trying to protect. I regretted the words, but couldn't take them back.

The low sun bathed the yard in brass-colored light. He finished mowing and said, unhappily, "You can make your own decision. But I don't want you to go. I don't want something to happen to you."

I gave in. I had already hurt him once with my words, and didn't want to do it again by defying him. All day in school, I felt like a coddled baby, because my two best friends had gone to the city.

The news that night reported that a mob of construction workers had attacked the protesters in front of the statue of George Washington at Federal Hall. They broke through the police line and chased everyone with long hair. They hit them with their hard hats and kicked them with their steel-toed boots. Seventy people had been injured.

I called Scott. Neither he nor Ira had long hair, and they were quick on their feet. Neither of them had gotten hurt.

I was glad that I hadn't gotten my skull cracked, and ashamed that I was glad. The fact that Dad had been right was hard to swallow.

He never said a word about it. And I never apologized for implying that he was a coward. I regretted it more and more as the years passed. I hoped he'd forgotten, but doubted it.

I had put him in an impossible bind. If he'd explained that he had once broken the law to protect a friend, I never would have insulted him again. But then he would have had to tell me that he had gone to prison.

Ellen's hand found mine under the table.

"Here's another question," I said. "He was always telling jokes with his friends. He seemed happy. Was that real? Because how do you just leave three years in prison behind?"

"That's who Morris was," Ruth said. "When we were kids, he was always cheerful, no matter what. He bounced back fast."

Her answer reminded me of something else: their loyalty to each other. When she'd had breast cancer and Uncle Irv couldn't take off from work, Dad had cancelled his appointments and spent days in the hospital with her.

Ellen leaned close. "The picture," she murmured.

I'd forgotten. I took the photo of Dad and Silvia from my shirt pocket. "Do any of you know anything about this girl?"

"*Mamzer*!" Goldie shouted.

Ruth said, "Will you stop? You always assume the worst."

"You think he was perfect. He wasn't close to perfect."

Irv said, "We met lots of people over there. It doesn't mean anything. I got invited to dinner a couple times. They loved us because we kicked out the Germans."

I studied the picture again. Irv's explanation didn't convince me. "It would be understandable," I said, "if he met someone and had a romance. He was young."

Sam said, "Naw. He was too crazy about your mother. Especially back then."

They weren't going to yield. I let it go.

Another question occurred to me: who clipped the articles? It didn't seem like something my mother would have done.

"That was me," Ruth said. "I didn't know if he'd want them, but I saved them just in case."

"Since we're telling him everything," Goldie said, "he should know a few more things. Your mother had plenty of reasons to be unhappy. She went through more than any of us."

Ruth, Irv, and Sam waited stoically.

"Rozzie had a baby before Paul—a stillbirth. They already had a cradle in the room. He painted giraffes and baby blocks on the wall. She was afraid to try again after that."

"It's true, that affected her for a long time," Ruth said.

"But there's something else. No one knows except me. Our father beat us. If we did something he didn't like, he would lock us in a dark closet."

Sam's aide had been slicing his chicken, making herself as invisible as possible. She shook her head.

"I was tough, but Rozzie wasn't. She cried the whole time. That's why she grew up scared of everything. I would stick my fingers under the door for her to hold. But if he caught me, he would get out his leather whip."

Ruth said, "Goldie, we had no idea."

"You all blamed her for years! You thought he was perfect and she just dragged him down."

The story helped explain something I've never understood. When Paul and Holly and I talk about our mother, we sometimes call her *tripolar*. My aunts and uncles know about her depression, but I doubt they know about the other two extremes. She could also be tender and affectionate—when she read *Horton Hatches the Egg* to me, she stroked my hair so lovingly—but minor mishaps would send her into sobbing hysterics. Our apartment had a washing machine in the kitchen, and you had to hook the drain hose over the edge of the sink; one time she forgot and it flooded the floor. She wailed and wept as she mopped it up, as if she were mopping the blood of her murdered family. At times like those, she terrified me.

Ellen said, "I'd like to say something positive about her. She had empathy for anyone in the world who suffered. I think she passed some of that down to Ken."

The dual compliment won approving nods from Ruth, Irv, and Sam. I found it embarrassing and not particularly deserved. "I wish they hadn't kept so many secrets," I said.

"They didn't want their problems to touch you," Ruth said. "The style now is to be more open, but that's how we did things then."

Sam patted my hand. "I think they made the right decision. You turned out good."

Julius dabbed his mouth with his napkin and looked into my eyes. "Your father was a fine man," he said. The words were barely audible.

I couldn't remember the last time he'd spoken to me. It may have been the 1970s. "Thank you, Julius."

"You're welcome."

I've never hugged and kissed my aunts and uncles. That's not our way. As they headed out of the restaurant, though—with a walker, a cane, a wheelchair—I understood that I should say a more meaningful goodbye than usual. So I went to them, one by one, put my arms around their shoulders, and kissed each one on the cheek: Sam, who enlisted just in time to fight in the Battle of Okinawa; Irv, who supervised the construction of a dozen Manhattan office buildings; Ruth, who helped low-income high school students get into college for three decades; Goldie, who raised my cousins Larry and Jack on her own after her first husband died.

Sam's bristles scratched my face, just like my father's had in his last years. Goldie's hair smelled like Mom's used to: Aqua Net, I think.

We went our separate ways in the parking lot. Sam waved to me from his wheelchair. Goldie moved carefully with her walker, concentrating. Irv leaned hard on his four-footed cane,

holding his free hand out for balance. "Look at my family,"
Ruth murmured.

I held her hand. She squeezed mine.

୨୦

On the way to the airport, I tried to picture my father defending
a small Puerto Rican man from a bunch of bigger soldiers. And
I had lectured him about courage.

"That was a lot of news at once," Ellen said.

"Mm-hm. But I still wonder if the other guy was really innocent."

"Does it matter? Your father believed what his friend said
and tried to help him. Isn't that what's important?"

Yes and no, I thought. One way, he was a noble soul who
did his best to protect an innocent man and paid a price for it.
The other way, he was a chump, a nice guy who suffered for his
gullibility. I respected his decency either way. But I hoped he
hadn't fallen for a lie.

Only one person would know. The odds that German Rosario is still alive are slim, but if he is, I have a few questions
for him.

4

We were at the airport, waiting to board. While Ellen dog-eared recipes in a magazine, I looked up German Rosario and found listings in New Jersey, on Staten Island, all over Florida, and up and down the East Coast.

I tried to think of a reason why my father would have risked so much to help him. The theory I came up with was that Rosario had saved Dad's life. When my father was lying wounded in the mountains, maybe Rosario was the one who searched and found him: repayment for the times when Dad had stood with him against the bullies.

Who would know? Not Ruth and Sam—they'd have mentioned it at lunch. But Snow Weiss might. He was Dad's best friend, ever since grammar school.

(It's interesting that they stayed close. I don't think my father ever broke a law—with one major exception—but Snow always had an angle. He needed money on top of his paycheck, Dad once told me, money that Betty didn't know about, so he could gamble. Among other scams, he used to punch guys in at work when they weren't there, in exchange for a few bucks. He never had an employer he didn't cheat, according to Dad. But the one who ended up in prison was the straight arrow.)

I found him online. *Seymour Weiss* in Boca Raton.

We had never spoken one to one. Like my aunts and uncles, he fell silent when I explained why I'd called. I told him I'd already talked to them and knew pretty much everything.

"I thought he was crazy not to tell you," Snow said. "But he didn't want to think about it ever again. He said, 'The subject is closed.'"

I told him my theory about Rosario saving my father's life. He said, "You got it backwards. Morris saved the other guy's life."

That confused me.

"He got shot a few days before your father did. Morris gave him first aid and carried him back."

Dad had never mentioned this to Snow, not until he was out on bail before the trial. Snow asked him, "Why the hell did you do it?" and Dad explained the whole history. "They say when you save someone's life, you feel a bond. I guess that's what happened."

I tried to picture my father hoisting another man onto his shoulder. The only part I could see clearly was the helmets, familiar from all those movies.

While I had Snow on the phone, I asked about Silvia. "Did he ever mention her? Do you know if they had a relationship? Or was she just someone he happened to meet?"

"Sorry, I can't help you there."

When I told Ellen about my father rescuing Rosario, she said, "Wow—Morris. What a guy!"

"I've waited my whole life to hear that story."

She already knew this, but I explained it again: how my father had seemed to grow smaller and smaller once I reached my teens. In later years, my disrespect had seemed traitorous to me. These stories about Rosario completely changed my idea of my father, and that relieved some of the bad feeling.

"He carried around so many secrets for so long," she said. "What a weight that must have been."

By comparison to what I now knew about my father, my own history looked shamefully comfortable. He had risked so much. Had I ever risked anything?

"You've got a lot to tell Ian and Evan," she said.

"Mm-hm."

As we rolled our bags down the jetway, I watched Ellen's gray curls bounce. She has been unfailingly supportive ever since Charlotte called. She isn't always this patient—not when I forget something on the shopping list, or when the people she's supervising do stupid things and get sent to jail—but she has been selfless these past few days.

From behind, there's no black left in her hair. I thought of the first time I'd seen her, at the pool in Florida: the wet, dark ponytail stuck to her back as she played with a baby, dunking him up to the waist and lifting him up high. She had blue eyes and pale skin: framed by black hair, it's a look I've always fallen for. Too bad she's already married, I thought. Then her sister waded over and took the baby, and they left the pool. Oh well, I told myself, that's that.

The following year, I saw her at the pool again, this time with an old woman in a white bathing cap. Her dark one-piece bathing suit made her look ghostly pale, but I liked what I saw. Once my father stopped kibitzing with friends, I asked if he knew the woman in the bathing cap. Of course he did—he knew everybody. He figured out quickly why I wanted to know. "I could introduce you," he said. I turned down the offer because I'd come down with Angela, my girlfriend of the moment, who was shopping for a beach hat with my mother. Dad told me to let him know if I changed my mind: his gentle way of suggesting that Ellen looked like a better match than Angela, who had already argued with him stridently about America's dirty hands in Iran and the unacceptable risks of nuclear power as proven by Three Mile Island.

I didn't manage to speak to Ellen until the following December. "You're in luck," Dad said as he drove me from the airport. "That girl you like broke up with her boyfriend. She's a probation officer." While hunched-over figures played cards in the shade and young fathers splashed with their kids, Dad and I sat together at the edge of the pool, watching Ellen swim laps. She glanced toward us a couple times, and I turned my head away. When she and her mother wandered over to chat, I wanted so much to make the right impression that I could barely speak. Our parents drew us in with their easy small talk, though. Later, we learned that they had conspired in advance without either of us knowing. They had even coordinated our visits.

It bothered me for a long time that I couldn't find a mate without my father's help. Now I'm just grateful. I owe him everything.

Cotton-ball clouds cast black shadows on the glittering water below us. I thought the shadows were islands at first.

The flight attendants served us pretzels, Cheez-Its, coffee, and wine. Ellen chatted with the young woman next to her while I sketched some thoughts in my notebook on the Home Care quality control project. Gerardo said he wants future reports to show opening and closing balances each month; I'd like to avoid changing the data request. But we should be able to provide the numbers fairly easily. If we count cases at the beginning of one month, and add new cases received, and subtract cases completed, then we'll have the month's closing balance, which equals the next month's opening balance. Counting cases will be laborious, but we'll only have to do it once.

Ellen's head was tipped back against her seat when I looked up. She was snoring, mouth open just slightly. The long, straight line of her nose was horizontal, elegant. Her bottom teeth, not usually visible, have grown more crooked over the years. If I hadn't met her, I thought, my life would have been a wasteland.

I looked forward to telling my sons everything I'd learned about their grandfather. That led to darker thoughts, though—a stream that flowed on and on. No matter how urgent Evan's work crisis, he would have come to the funeral if he didn't resent me. But why does he? I never abused him. He was born this way, hypersensitive and prone to hold grudges.

I wasn't a perfect father. I didn't spend as much time with them as I could have, and when I did, my mind often wandered. But Ian grew up in the same house and he seems nostalgic about his childhood.

There was a period when Evan and I flew kites in the park together and kayaked on the Delaware. For a while, he preferred me to Ellen. But he changed in middle school. He chose reckless friends who challenged each other to jump off garage roofs. In high school, he turned into a brooder, always in his own head, never really with us. I prodded him too much, trying to get him to try harder in school and not waste so much time. My comments irritated him—"Is there any chance you'll ever read a book again?"—but he has no idea how many I kept to myself.

Ian brought his whole family to Florida. Evan didn't even call, he just sent a two-line email saying he couldn't make it because of work. It was a strong statement.

Change of subject.

How I imagine German Rosario: a frail man in a nursing home, slumped over a table in the dining room, hard of hearing, confused—but then I say, *I'm Morris Weintraub's son.* He stares into my eyes, and remembers. He offers a hand to shake. And then I ask, *When you said it wasn't you who tried to shoot that congressman, were you telling the truth?*

The hand slips away. His focus shifts. He no longer sees me.

After unpacking, Ellen turned on her exercise music and took over the bedroom. Prince sang, "Let's Go Crazy," and her bare feet thudded on the floor. I'm not sure why we've never gotten an enraged call from downstairs.

The apartment felt a little empty. We usually go our separate ways after dinner—she goes to the gym or talks to friends on the phone, I read the *Times* on my stationary bike or struggle through an article in *Corriere della Sera*, to keep up my feeble Italian—but I didn't want to leave her after these days together.

(I'd like to break our habit of spending the evenings apart. I'd like to be closer.)

In my office, I lifted the cover of the big Strathmore drawing pad. Turning the pages, I found arms nearly as long as legs, and only the most timid suggestions of muscle definition. I'm wasting my time—but I already knew that. Art is not the pursuit that will enrich the last quarter of my life. I should keep searching.

One drawing stopped me. The model had bent like a jack-knife and grasped his ankles, a thirty-second pose. It reminded me of what Charlotte told me about Dad's last conscious moments. He'd had stomach pain for a few days, so they made an appointment with his doctor. But as Joyce helped him into the car, he suddenly bent over and passed out. After that, he never came to.

He'd had a stomach infection, she told me. They had waited too long. If they'd gone to the doctor a day earlier, he might still be alive.

It may have been his own fault. He always minimized his pain. He must have kept it to himself until he couldn't stand it.

To die without knowing you're dying: some people think that's the best way to go. To me, it's tragic. When my time comes, I hope I know what's going on. I hope I'll have reached a place of acceptance. It seems achievable.

But it must be harder when it's really happening to you.

Evan came to apologize, and left everything worse than before.

He's lost weight. The purple shadows under his eyes have darkened. But he still has a smoother baby face than any adult I know.

He drove across the Brooklyn Bridge and through the Holland Tunnel because Ian told him I was upset. I think Ian must have gone further than that. *What's your fucking problem? Why do you treat him like shit? It's not acceptable.*

I said, "I appreciate your coming. I know you've got a lot going on." All of which was true: his wife is going to have a baby soon, and he's in the middle of shooting a documentary. For the first few minutes, just seeing him made up for everything.

The three of us sat at the dinner table. We couldn't persuade him to eat or drink. He said he's having problems with the main on-camera subject of his film. Unless he works it out, he'll lose his funding. He spent the last three days in Montana, pleading with the guy. He can't afford to let this project fall apart.

Ellen asked what the problem was. He didn't want to go into details.

"Did you work it out?" I asked.

"For now. But I don't trust this guy. He's paranoid—and he has reason to be. He may be risking his life."

He has kept the subject of this film secret, but tonight he let us in on it. "You've heard about white supremacists infiltrating police departments, right? I'm working with some local reporters, documenting stories. But we keep running into roadblocks. I'm sick of the whole thing."

He stared somberly at the bowl of fruit between us: the perfect oranges, the brown-spotted bananas. He was irritated and unhappy, but I was proud of him. He's doing more valuable work than I ever thought he would.

"Aren't you taking a risk?" Ellen asked. "These are violent people."

He said he's been keeping a low profile. Then he asked, "So, how was the funeral?"

Ellen told him I had delivered a beautiful eulogy. He said he was sorry he missed it. I promised to send him the text.

We were treating him like the Prodigal Son, but he looked like he would rather have been anywhere else.

To distract him from his distraction, I asked if he remembered going to Disney World with Grandpa and me. "Of course," he said. Nostalgia suffuses that memory: Ian and Evan at the fort on Tom Sawyer's Island, aiming rifles through a sharpshooter's slit each time the mine train came clacking by. Dad telling me how smart they both seemed.

A spasm of grief seized me. Dodging it, I said, "Getting through the eulogy was harder than I expected. I had to keep looking up at Mommy and Ian to steady myself."

He studied the sumi-e painting of the stretching cat, which is new. "Would you like me to build a time machine so I can go back and be there?"

"I wasn't accusing you."

He let out a harsh hiccup of a laugh.

Ellen said, "We're glad you came over. Let's look forward to the baby instead of dwelling on the past."

"Sure. Let's."

I said, "I know you would have come if you could."

The straw placemat in front of him held his attention for several seconds. Then he said, "You're being diplomatic. Admit it: you'll remember forever that I didn't show up."

It's a compulsion, I thought. A ritual. We can't escape.

"Or," Ellen said, "we could say that sometimes you can't do what your father wants you to, and you feel bad about it, and you end up snapping at him."

I was grateful for the help.

"I'll accept that," Evan said. "But what I said is still true."

"What's your grievance, exactly?" I asked. "That I wish you'd come to the funeral? Or is it something else?"

He pulled his mouth all the way to one side. I understood that I shouldn't have asked the question.

"I'll just say one thing. You were always lecturing me, pushing me to work harder and choose a career that mattered. But what about you? Why didn't you take your own advice?"

Some toast crumbs lay near the edge of the table. I watched my fingers corral them into a small triangle.

He's such a cog, he once said to Ian. They were in the kitchen and didn't realize I was in the basement, within earshot. His casual contempt murdered me. I had no defense: long ago I had imagined myself as a prosecutor, bringing corporate villains to justice, but one semester of law school was all I could take. I never believed I would someday rouse a jury with my righteous passion. Instead, I followed my talent and temperament and studied computer programming—a reasonable choice, but not the kind that impresses a teenage son.

Ellen defended me again. "Do you have any idea how many people depend on Medicaid in the city? Something like three million. It takes a lot of people to make the system work. And he's an important one."

He let it go. For me, that was harder to do. I've wanted to find more exciting work for years. Every time the DOI uncovers a major fraud, or police abuse, or even a failure by NYCHA to inspect lead paint, I think, *I should have gone to work for them.*

"I'd better get going," he said.

Ellen followed him to the door. "You'll let us know as soon as Erin has the baby, right?"

He must have answered, but I couldn't hear it.

I expected her to apportion the blame evenly between us,

but only my share mattered to her. "Good job. A really excellent fuck-up."

"I asked him one question."

The lines in her forehead deepened. She looked sinister. "You know what he's like. What if he decides he doesn't want us to help with the baby?"

"Am I supposed to censor every word out of my mouth?"

"With him, yes!"

Rage swelled inside me, sudden and hot.

"Everything in my life is frustrating me right now," she said. "This is the one thing I've been looking forward to."

"Please don't say *everything* when you mean certain specific things."

"I mean everything."

Instead of shouting, I went to the door. But it wasn't enough just to leave. I took an orange from the bowl on the table and hurled it as hard as I could, through the kitchen doorway and against the wall. The skin split; bits of pulp flew everywhere, juice splattered up and down the wall. Thin fingers of liquid trickled down toward the molding. The orange rolled back toward us, exposing a crack like a wicked smile.

I left the mess for her to clean up.

(No, it wasn't a relief to let the anger out. I felt like an ass. And I was still furious.)

At the river, I leaned on the railing and wrote to Dave, my college roommate. *I was a jerk just now,* I said. *But I was provoked.* I told the story in brief, and also let him know about my father.

Watching the boats go by calmed me somewhat. But I couldn't imagine returning to the apartment.

Dave was working at home. *I'm very sorry about your dad. I've thought of him more times than I can count. He always seemed like the best guy in the world—so sweet and funny and unassuming. I envied you a lot.*

(The fondness had been mutual. Dad liked Dave best of all my college friends. For every joke Dad told, Dave knew two others with the same cast of characters—dogs in bars, rabbis and priests, old people arriving in heaven. Dave became an entertainment lawyer in L.A., and Dad loved to hear about his celebrity clients.)

About Ellen, he wrote, *Nothing will help except time, and an apology. You wouldn't be human if you never lost your temper. I assume things will be uncomfortable for a few days. It might help to replace the orange.*

I snorted. A young couple to my left glanced my way, making sure they didn't need to put more space between us.

As for Evan, Dave suggested I send an email, saying more or less the following: *Nothing is more important to me than you and your brother. In a way, I'm glad we had that little blow-up, because it gives me a chance to tell you that I love you.*

I'm not going to take that advice—it's not the kind of language Evan and I use with each other—but reading his words comforted me, and I told him so.

I didn't want to keep him from his work, so I said I needed to go to home and sleep, because some of us have to get up in the morning—a reference to my favorite Dave joke, about the guy who finds out he only has one night to live, so he goes home and tells his wife, and they make love twice, but she says no to a third time, because some of us have to get up in the morning.

All of the lights were out except the little red one on the TV. Ellen wasn't snoring, so I knew she was still awake.

I would have slept on the couch, but I tried that once and didn't fall asleep till four. Tomorrow I return to work. I don't want to nod out at my desk.

After undressing in the living room, I entered the room as quietly as I could. Praying she wouldn't lash out at me, I climbed into bed. She was on her side, with her back to me. I lay down in the same position, facing away from her.

She didn't speak. It was what I'd hoped for, but her silence seemed spiteful and unfair.

I thought about Genevieve, the philosophy professor. I could arrange a visit to check on Charlotte—just me. I could contact Genevieve and ask if she'd like to have dinner. Why don't I cook something? she says. I saw myself driving a rental car to her home, a condo with a balcony and a view of the ocean. She greets me at the door in a ribbed white tank top. (We seem to be twenty years younger here.) Wine with dinner... I help carry the dishes in... not sure what to do then... she turns and leans back against the sink, facing me. She asks, Would it be okay if I kissed you?... Now I have a decision to make. While I'm hesitating, she touches my beard, and traces my lips with a fingertip.

It seemed very real, very possible—and therefore terrifying.

5

Before I made it to my cubicle, half of my group jumped up from their chairs to offer condolences. Most were nervous and awkward—"So, he must have been, like, pretty old, right?"—but I understood. I've been in their shoes often enough.

On my desk stood a nubby glass vase with white roses and lilies, and a card, *We're all thinking of you.* Everyone had signed the card, but I knew who had organized the whole thing. It could only have been Myriam.

Dermot had called a meeting for nine-thirty. He rarely meets with my whole team, so I knew there was a problem. I chose not to worry.

They had all taken their places at the conference table before I arrived. I thanked them for the flowers. "You're okay?" Edwin asked. I said, "My father had a long life and a lot of friends. You can't ask for much more." They nodded soberly, but the words sounded formulaic to me. Though I try not to spout platitudes, sometimes they slip out before I can stop them. "It's good to see you all again," I said.

Dermot grew up in Dublin, the son of a banker. Gruff and remote, he's uncomfortable with social niceties. He strode in with shoulders forward, hunched like a cartoon buzzard, pre-occupied. "Ken, so sorry to hear about your father," he said.

I thanked him and we got down to business. The problem was this: the number my unit reported for Medicaid-eligible Bronx residents is twelve percent higher than the number the State D.O.H. reported. Based on recent history, their number looks right, and that's a big discrepancy. "The mayor is suspicious. He thinks we may be cherry-picking the numbers to get more resources. I had to swear it was a simple mistake."

His face flushed as he said this. You could see the anger simmering.

"I want this fixed today," he said. "And I want to know who's responsible."

He could have figured out that Bogdan had done the report, since that was the only name cc'd on my cover memo, but he hasn't caught on to my system. Bogdan started eight months ago and has made other mistakes, but I've always caught them before this. He was sitting two seats away from me. I could see, through the glass tabletop, one hand massaging the other in his lap.

I wanted to tell Dermot, *Don't come in here and terrorize my team. People make mistakes.*

Policing myself, I kept my voice flat. "Let me look through the report. As soon as I find the error, I'll draft a memo explaining what happened. You can either forward it to the mayor or put it in your own words. Let's just fix it and move on."

Dermot's head tipped forward as if sagging under its own weight. Let him write me up, I thought. I've been here too long as it is.

Perhaps because I'm fifteen years older than he is, or because my father just died, he let go of his little inquisition. "Just make sure you get it right." His distrustful glare touched every face in the room. "Be more careful from now on. I'm not as forgiving as Ken. And I don't want the mayor to call me ever again."

"We'll do our best," I said.

We watched through the glass wall as he lumbered toward the elevators. "We're done in here," I told them. "Bogdan, just stay for a minute."

As they filed out, a couple of them patted my shoulder.

Bogdan wouldn't look at me. He may have thought I was going to tell him to look for another job.

"Let me see what happened," I said, "and then we'll go over it together." I didn't want to criticize him after what he'd just gone through, but his sloppiness had put me in an unpleasant spot. "I agree with Dermot on one point: please be more careful in the future."

He nodded, nodded, nodded, and left.

I had looked forward to returning to everyday life, but Dermot's crisis upended that. With no space for daydreaming, I set to work.

First I checked the query conditions, assuming I'd find the mistake there. No luck. Bogdan had set up the parameters perfectly.

Since this was likely to take all morning, I went to the kitchen and reheated a cup of coffee. As I sat down, the mug bumped against my armrest and spilled half its contents. *My brain is disintegrating*, I thought as the coffee seeped into the carpet.

Back to the kitchen for a roll of paper towels. After placing the white squares on the wet places, I pressed them down with my shoe and considered retiring early—maybe next year. It would mean taking reduced Social Security benefits, but I may not have as much time left as I assume. When I run on a treadmill, I have chest pains (though a cardiogram showed nothing) and my teeth seem to break every time I eat an almond. (Three crowns so far, and no more almonds.)

In the end, I had to squat and press new paper towels against the carpet by hand. That's when Myriam stopped by.

She helped, of course. While we blotted coffee together, she said, "I just wanted to make sure you're okay."

"I'm fine."

"You didn't even look nervous in there. I was scared to death."

"There was nothing to be worried about, really."

Reading from her phone, she said I should scrub the carpet with a mixture of water, Palmolive, and vinegar. But the carpet is charcoal gray, and I couldn't see a stain. I said I'd probably leave it alone.

"I also wanted to ask how you're doing," she said. "Because of your father."

I invited her to take a seat. Work still has its small satisfactions, and Myriam is one of them. She's like a daughter—a lovely, admiring, untroubled daughter. No one looks up to me the way she does.

She's very close with her parents, she told me. She talks to them a few times a day, and can't imagine losing one of them. I told her that, although I loved my father, we didn't have that kind of relationship.

Myriam wears a crucifix. Her family is Lebanese, but her father, a doctor, moved them to Buenos Aires when she was small. He died when she was a teenager and her mother moved the family to New Jersey to be close to her sisters. Myriam is religious, Maronite Catholic, which means that her beliefs about the universe are as far from mine as they could possibly be. But I can talk to her more comfortably than I can talk to most of my friends.

I told her what I'd learned about my father's crime and punishment, and remembered the two letters. "I have to deal with that Bronx report, but could I ask a favor first? My father saved a couple letters in Spanish. I was hoping you could translate them."

I fished the small creased page out of the first envelope. She pushed her glasses closer to her eyes. I recorded her voice.

In the first letter—the one from 1945, addressed to my father at Muller's—German Rosario's mother thanked Dad again and again for saving her son's life. "He was always small and quiet. He was born a month early, we didn't know if he would survive. It wasn't easy for him—the bigger ones picked on him. But I believe God had a purpose for him because He preserved him through everything. I believe that God worked through your hands. Now he is at home again, with a job, and soon he will marry a good girl. God has blessed me.

"He doesn't speak about the army. He said there were some bad men and some good ones. He mentioned you and someone named Fred. I think perhaps you helped him other times, before he was wounded. If it was that way, then I thank you a thousand times more.

"If you need help or prayers, depend on us. May the Lord bless you and your family.

"Nydia Rosario."

Fred was Fred Stapleton. It occurred to me that the reason he

called my father that time must have been, not that he'd heard
Dad had survived the war, but that he found out his old friend
had gotten out of prison. The letter also raised a disturbing
possibility. German's mother said he had been bullied as a kid,
and my uncles said the same about his time in the army. That
kind of misery turns into rage; and sometimes rage expresses
itself with bullets. Dad tended to overlook people's faults. He
may have misjudged German Rosario.

Myriam usually speaks in a flute-like register, but as she read
the letter, her voice dropped to a lower place, soft and reverent.
She had tucked her hair behind her ears, but one dark lock freed
itself and fell past her lips and throat.

Confused longing gripped me. I loved Myriam like a daughter—like a best friend—like a woman I wished could love me.

She had no makeup on, and her glasses (two unstylish dark
ovals) made her look like a member of the high school math
team. To me, though, she was more appealing than any movie
star.

But she's the same age as Evan. She has a one-year-old
daughter. She goes to church every Sunday. And she looks at
me as a kindly teacher. I remember what sixty-one looks like
when you're thirty.

(Her first year, she made a mistake that resulted in a figure
more glaringly wrong than Bogdan's. I caught that one in time.
Looking over her query, I saw that she had failed to require
that both the individual and the case had to be active; she'd
only specified individuals, so her total included cases that were
closed. I had her run the report again, and we submitted it just
a half-hour late. She apologized, head down with shame and
remorse, as if she had accidentally hurt a child. Reassuring her,
I said I should have given her clearer instructions. I wouldn't say
that her eyes filled with tears, but there was mist in her gratitude.
She has thanked me with loyalty and friendship ever since.)

"Your father must have helped his friend a lot," she said. "It
sounds like he had a beautiful heart."

"I didn't know about any of this. I wish he'd told me while
he was alive."

I wanted to add that I'd never noticed what a lovely voice she has, but I didn't, for fear that she'd see what lurked behind the compliment.

She asked how my father had saved German's life. I told her what I knew.

"No wonder his mother was grateful. My mom would have written the same letter."

I had to look away. There, push-pinned to the cubicle divider, was Ellen in a field of yellow tulips. Holland, 2008.

"You're lucky you're so close to your parents," I said. "Emotionally and geographically."

"That's not luck. I told my husband we couldn't move more than fifteen minutes away."

"You never argue with them?"

"I get annoyed sometimes. She keeps telling me I should pierce Alissa's ears, and I'm not sure. But that's so unimportant."

I wished I could keep her with me. The error in the Bronx report had to be found and fixed, though. And the worst of my madness had passed. "I should get to work on those numbers for Dermot. Thanks for translating the letter. Maybe we can do the other one a different time."

She bent to hug my shoulders before she left, something she has never done before. I held her arm, in a fatherly way.

I had hoped to look up German Rosario at the library on my lunch hour, but it took till noon to find the error in the Bronx report. (Examining the data again, I saw that these numbers couldn't have been generated using the conditions Bogdan had shared with me. We studied the actual query together at his computer, and he noticed that he'd accidentally deleted a key restriction: his report included clients who had applied but not yet been approved.) I asked him to correct the query and run it again. By the time I had reviewed the new report and drafted the cover memo—assuring the mayor that the mistake had originated in a minor oversight by one of the analysts, which I had failed to spot—it was four-fifteen. I sent it to Dermot and went upstairs to make sure he was satisfied.

"You're confident this one is accurate?" he asked. I told him, "The total matches the D.O.H. figure now."

He let out a skeptical *hm*. I don't think he really suspected me of copying the other number, but that seemed to be the implication.

I wanted many things. I wanted help locating a person with a fairly common name, who once went to prison for a newsworthy crime. I wanted to learn how long he spent behind bars. And I wanted to see what the newspaper columnists and letter writers had said about the attempted assassination.

This was going to require microfilm. I took the subway up to Forty-Second Street.

The library keeps its microfilm in long file cabinets organized by newspaper and date. I gathered the reels from the *Post*, the *Herald Tribune*, the *Daily News*, and the *Daily Mirror* for the days after the shooting. Threading the film around the rollers and between the glass plates sent me back to high school, to the main library in Jamaica, where I'd gone to research the conflict in Northern Ireland for a term paper.

Green light spilled from inside the machine. As I fast-forwarded through the pages, the whir harmonized with a siren on the street. The newsprint blurred: the classified ads turned gray, the comics left airier spaces. (I couldn't help pausing to see what the world had looked like the year I was born. For fifty-five dollars, a woman could get a "Hand-Tailored Suit" at Alexander's. Robert Hall and S. Klein still existed. I hadn't heard those names in a long time.)

There wasn't much commentary on the Powell incident, only columns by Westbrook Pegler and Walter Lippmann and a few letters in the *Post* and *Daily News*. Lippmann spent most of his column spewing facts about the attempt on Powell's life and the Capitol shootings a few days earlier. The details implied a portrait of a disorganized, incompetent movement. It was interesting to learn that the Puerto Ricans who fired at the floor of the House of Representatives all lived in New York City (in other words, whoever shot at Powell may have been connected with them) and that the woman who had led the Capitol attack had placed a note in her purse that read, *My life I give for the freedom of my country*—an echo of Nathan Hale. One congressman tied his necktie around a colleague's leg to stop the bleeding. Lippmann expressed sympathy for colonial subjects who yearn for independence, but wrote that *until the majority of the population fervently supports the cause—which most Puerto Ricans do not—the revolutionaries are doomed to fail. Authorities will crush the rebellion and blood will be shed pointlessly. When these freedom fighters can show they have the people behind them, they should bring their case to Washington again—and leave their guns home.*

Pegler, who had earned fame as a vicious critic of FDR—and who had perfected the art of deranged right-wing mudslinging long before Alex Jones, et al.—assumed that Soviet influence lay behind the attacks. *Is any "independence" movement in our backyard likely to be independent of Moscow's puppet masters, or of the reds in our own sordid "labor movement"? Send the bloodhounds on the trail of Puerto Rico's Nationalist Party and I'll bet my eye teeth they'll sniff out a comradely rendezvous or two with Kremlin operatives. Meanwhile, our pink press yowls about the purported excesses of "McCarthyism." We were a great and free nation, until 1933. Now we harass and scapegoat the valiant few who seek to carve out the cancer.*

A *Daily News* editorial dismissed the independence fighters as *oddies.* One letter writer, Albert Colon, pleaded poignantly for Americans to understand that most Puerto Ricans considered the shooters criminals and wanted nothing to do with their cause. "I fought for the U.S. in the Pacific. I will always defend my country from harm, even if it comes from those of my own background."

Other letters bluntly insulted Rosario and my father. Salvatore Russo from the Bronx wrote, *Are more attacks in the works? Are we going to see Puerto Ricans firing their pistols every time an official steps out in public? I say the FBI should put pressure on these gunmen until they break. Let's find out what they've got planned. Public safety demands it.* James J. Quinlan Jr., from Sunnyside, wrote, *That island isn't worth the trouble it's causing us. Let them go. They have nothing to do with us. We live by the law, they live by the gun. Let them have their independence, they can enjoy the same poverty as their neighbors. And any Puerto Rican residents of the 48 states who don't appreciate what they've got here are welcome to go home.* Arnold Fishman, from Maspeth, vented his outrage fiercely. *It's not surprising to see a hothead try to settle a dispute with a revolver. But what kind of American hides a foreign assassin from the police? He says they were army buddies. So what? I fought in the same war, and I would never shield a would-be murderer. Morris Weintraub, you've done no favors for your country, or your people.*

Their contempt surprised me. Four people in my department are Puerto Rican. I don't think of them as belonging to a despised minority, though I know Latinos lag behind whites in income and education. My colleagues seem as American to me as anyone else in the office. But it was different then. A *Post* editorial, published a day before the letters, predicted the attitude of the three New Yorkers with startling accuracy: "Tragically, we can now expect the know-nothings to raise their voices once again and blame all our problems on our immigrant neighbors from Puerto Rico." For my father to stand by Rosario, to shield him from the law—especially with the *Daily News* shouting *MANHUNT* over a police sketch—required not just courage, but immunity to the bigotry that had infected so many others.

I was proud of him, and amazed.

Rosario's mother made her son sound like a frail man, without friends. It was hard to imagine him bearing up under the weight of a trial and imprisonment.

I searched for his name together with Adam Clayton Powell's, in order to learn how many years he'd spent behind bars. An article from 1956, two years after the shooting, said that he had been beaten to death by fellow inmates at the U.S. Penitentiary in Atlanta.

The article was short and gave few details. According to the warden, a group of Negro prisoners had assaulted Rosario, punching and kicking him. The cause of death was reported as internal bleeding. Prison authorities assumed that the assailants had learned of Rosario's crime—the attempted assassination of one of only two Negroes in Congress—and conspired to take revenge.

Film spun from spool to spool on the machines around me. Of all the facts presented, the one that dug its claws deepest into me was Rosario's size: five foot five, one hundred and twenty pounds.

So small. So thin.

6

People were hurrying up and down Fifth Avenue. I turned the corner and found the only empty table in Bryant Park.

I looked up Fred Stapleton first, because I remembered him. He took us fishing once. The five of us crowded into his rowboat; in order for us all to fit, Paul and Dad had to share the middle seat and row together. I remember the morning fog on the hills around us. Fred was soft-spoken and tall. When Dad handed me the fishing pole, Fred said, "Hold on tight. Don't let a fish steal it out of your hands." He told me to give the rod a good tug if I felt a bite, to set the hook.

Fred died in 1977, I learned. According to the *Sun Bulletin* obituary, he graduated from Johnson City High school in 1943, enlisted immediately, and went to work in his father's exterminating business after the war. He was an active member of the Sarah Jane Johnson Memorial United Methodist Church, and was ordained a deacon in 1949. His wife, Fenna, survived him.

I found a listing for her on Grand Boulevard in Binghamton. Hoping she could tell me whatever stories Fred had told her, I called her number. Our conversation was strained. She still has a faint accent, and she didn't offer sympathy when she heard that my father had died. ("Do you remember him?" "Of course. I remember you too.") I explained that my parents had kept many secrets and left me with many questions. She said she doubted she could answer them. Fred had never talked about the war.

I should have given up at that point, but I wanted to know about Dad's friendship with Fred. She reluctantly agreed to a brief visit over the weekend, a plan I regretted as soon as I hung up. I had just committed to more than six hours of driving on a Sunday in August, to speak with a woman who wanted nothing to do with me.

After that, I was less eager to call Rosario's widow. A few Marquita Rosarios were listed in the United States and Puerto Rico, but only one was over eighty. The address was in Mount Vernon, New York, relatively close.

The man who answered had a rough, friendly voice. "Rosario—what's up?" When I told him I was trying to reach Marquita Rosario, he went quiet. "She's not with us anymore. Who's this?"

I told him my name. "My father was a friend of her husband's," I said.

"You said Weintraub?" he asked cautiously.

"Yes."

"Is your father Morris?"

I'd reached Oscar, Rosario's son. He kept me on the phone for twenty minutes, telling me how much his family owed to my dad. "Your pop's name is like a legend for us," he said.

Each of us had lost a parent in the last month. "It sucks, right?"

Every door I knocked on seemed to have a corpse behind it.

Impulsively, I told him I'd be driving past his town on Sunday night. Would he like me to stop by?

"*Please.* You have to."

Ellen was cutting chicken breasts in half when I got home. "What can I do?" I asked. She pointed with the tip of the poultry shears to the scallions on the cutting board.

We cooked without speaking, and listened to *All Things Considered.* When the show ended, she switched the radio off and we continued in silence.

I wanted to tell her what I'd learned at the library, and what Oscar had said. But those stories were important to me, too important to share if she meant to freeze me out. Instead I asked how her first day back at work had been. "Hectic," she said.

I didn't apologize for throwing the orange and she didn't apologize for blaming me. We said very few words, and separated after eating, as always.

Saturday wasn't much better. I told her I'd be driving upstate the next day, and why.

She was dressing for Pilates in the bedroom. All she said was, "You'll get caught in Sunday night traffic coming back from the Catskills."

Yes, I knew that.

Our silence has become an embarrassment to us both, I think.

"You realize," she said, "that no matter what anyone tells you, you'll never know what was inside your father's head."

I knew that too. "I just want to find out as much as I can. The more of the facts I can sort out, the more at peace I'll be."

She let out a skeptical sigh. "Enjoy the drive."

We've never had a falling-out that lasted this long. Driving up the Turnpike, I wondered if she sometimes wished she'd married someone else—someone more cheerful, or more exciting.

I listened to a biography of Frances Perkins for a while, but needed something more gripping to distract me. A Damon Runyon story accomplished the goal. After that, I let the radio scan from station to station for many miles. Finally I put on Keith Richards's memoir.

In the opening chapter, the Stones get stopped by cops in Arkansas. Their car is full of drugs, and they panic. They hide the stuff under the seat in a squashed Kleenex box and throw some of it out into the bushes. I laughed out loud.

Lost in the story, I missed my exit and had to drive back to Binghamton through Johnson City. That didn't bother me at all. I'd lived there when I was small and had gone to college a few miles away. I welcomed the chance to see it again.

Not much remained of what I remembered, except the old arch over Main Street—*Home of the Square Deal*—which I could still picture with snow piled on top. They had cleared away many of the buildings and hadn't gotten around to replacing them yet. The landscape was flat, bleak, and hot.

Fenna Stapleton's house was mustard-colored, an Addams

Family mansion, one of the grandest on Grand Boulevard. A fence enclosed the property; behind the black iron spears, tall hedges formed a second line of defense. The foundation plantings included black-eyed Susans, hostas with leaning stalks of purple bells, and many flowers I couldn't identify. The exterior paint had started to peel, but you couldn't see that until you reached the doorstep.

Fenna herself has grown lean and handsome, with a tan face softened by fine blonde down. Her home was eclectically decorated and immaculate. A ceiling fan turned in the living room, but she had no air conditioner. A bay window let in more sun than we needed on an August afternoon.

She served hot tea soon after I arrived, and brought out a round blue tin of Royal Dansk butter cookies. "I'm surprised at your age," she said. "I knew you had grown up, but I didn't realize how much."

The cookies were stale and hard. I dunked one in tea to avoid breaking a tooth.

Facts about her life:

Her parents smelled the danger from Germany and moved the family from Rotterdam to the Bronx in 1938.

Fred died of a heart attack when he was fifty-one. She hired a man to keep the appointments they already had scheduled. By appealing to members of their congregation and persuading local hardware stores to hand out a calling card, she attracted new customers.

She moved to this house in 1988, and sold the business in 2005, when she was seventy-eight. By then, she had four men working for her.

She attends the local philharmonic and opera. Until recently, she traveled for a month of every year. She has walked on every continent, including Antarctica.

They never had children. She didn't want to, because Fred drank. After a certain point, his mildness would turn to its opposite and he would shove or slap her. Later, he would apologize abjectly and promise never to do it again. But he was so gloomy and lifeless when he was sober, she couldn't bear it.

Her bluntness surprised me. She claimed to have liked my
father, but then she said that Dad talked too much with the
customers, and arrived late to his appointments. She wanted
Fred to fire him—they didn't have enough work to support two
families—but Fred wouldn't do it.

Steering us toward a safer topic, I asked about their friendship. They must have been close in the army if Fred had called
and offered Dad a job.

"Fred didn't offer him a job," she said. "Your father called
and asked for a job. The post office didn't want him back. And
Fred couldn't refuse, because he was such a good Christian. It
was charity, and we couldn't afford it."

The spite with which she said *good Christian* startled me. I
told her I was sorry for the trouble my family had caused her.
Then I asked if Fred had ever mentioned German Rosario, or
the bullying. She said she knew nothing about it.

"Apparently some men in their platoon kept picking on one
particular person. I've heard that my father tried to stop them
and Fred backed him up."

"It sounds like something he would do. Putting his nose in
other people's problems."

At that point I gave up hope of learning anything enlighten-
ing. "I shouldn't have bothered you," I said.

"It doesn't bother me to think of these things. He's been
gone forty years. I've had forty good years."

While I searched for a way to take my leave, she said, "You
want to hear that these were two wonderful men and great pals.
You won't hear that from me. They were very ordinary. And the
money worries made Fred drink even more."

I wanted to escape, but didn't want her to think I couldn't
bear her truth-telling.

She had stocked the room with an unusual assortment of
furnishings. The chairs had Navajo, African, and Indian uphol-
stery. A coffee table with bamboo legs stood on a red kilim.
Small, colorful pillows littered the couch like confetti. All of
this made a pleasantly bohemian impression, which bore no
relation whatsoever to her cold spirit.

She stared calmly into my eyes. "Would you like to know what really happened with your father?"

The implication that she'd been shielding me until now caught me off guard. "All right."

"Word got out that he had gone to prison. There were rumors he might be a Communist. Customers stopped using us. I told Fred that he had to fire Morris if we wanted to survive. He refused. So I talked to Morris. I explained that he was going to destroy our business unless he left. He understood—but he didn't quit, not for another year. I think he talked to Fred, and Fred told him to ignore me. But let me ask you this: was it right for him to do this to a friend? You want to think of your father as a fine man, but a fine man would have acted differently."

Punched in the gut, I tried to defend my father. "He'd just gotten out of prison. He was at a low point in his life. The job was his life raft."

"I know that. But I couldn't respect him afterwards."

Taking shelter, I thought of the first time my father brought me along on a job. The apartment was on a river, in a poor part of town, a place unlike any in Queens. We had to climb a creaky outdoor staircase over the water. He let me aim the wand as we walked along the edges of the kitchen. He was happy to have me with him. The customer, a man in a turban, called me a good boy. My father beamed.

"How does it help to dig up the past?" Fenna asked. "Does this information make you feel better?"

"I think most people, when they lose a parent, want to hear about the things they never knew. Good or bad."

"It would be healthier to live your own life."

The need to get away from her became overwhelming. It was like holding a fistful of ice: the sensation had gone past discomfort.

"I have to head back," I said, though I'd spent less than twenty minutes with her.

"Of course."

At the front door, I rebelled against the tyranny of politeness, in a small way. I said, "Thank you for your kindness."

If she heard my meaning, she didn't show it. "No trouble at all."

She closed the door behind me and locked both locks.

Perhaps because I didn't want to think about what Fenna had said, I paid a visit to the street where we'd once lived. The neighborhood had been poor back then—I understood that even when I was six—but it had gone far downhill. A shirtless white guy with a tattooed chest stood on Grand Avenue with a thinner, sickly-looking customer; they watched me drive past before finishing their transaction. A block away from our old apartment, a pair of cops had a different white guy sitting on the curb, handcuffed.

I turned on Hudson Street to look at the house. Back then the gray box had seemed ordinary to me. Nearly sixty years later, it looked like an emblem of American poverty. Holes and dents marked the siding. In front, on the sidewalk, bags of trash had fallen over next to a TV with a cracked screen.

Driving south on the highway, I tried to make sense of what I'd seen. People live this way all over America. The president said the other day that the economy is recovering (GDP grew almost 4 percent in the second quarter), but even a booming economy won't touch this neighborhood. If you wanted to do something valuable with your life, this would be the problem to solve. But how?

Fenna's words kept pressing in on my thoughts—*I couldn't respect him afterwards*—but I held them out.

The factory jobs disappeared around here long ago. You could give companies tax incentives to open new factories, but you couldn't hire those young guys without shirts. Generations of poverty have made them unemployable.

Where would it make sense to concentrate your efforts? What would Frances Perkins do?

Oscar Rosario and his wife, Cookie, live in a two-story apartment building in Mount Vernon. From the front, everything looked freshly painted and repaired, but the side of the building faced a curbless street of cracked pavement. Grass met the roadway in an uneven line of mud, pebbles, and silt.

Just as Ellen and I did, they moved to this apartment after their kids grew up and left home. Their place was smaller, though. The kitchen opened into the living room, with the dinner table straddling the border.

Oscar hugged me at his front door before we'd even finished shaking hands. He's only about five-six but he's muscular. The sleeves of his Hawaiian shirt barely fit around his arms.

Straight flat nose, short curly hair, irises like black marbles: there's no trace of Europe in his face. Severe acne left deep scars, but his smile is huge. He has dedicated his life to spreading positivity, he explained. Though not especially religious, he lives without drugs or alcohol and preaches the benefits of fitness and athletics to boys in trouble. A tattoo on his forearm says, *Never Too Late.*

The apartment smelled like fried fish. Cookie was clearing the dinner plates while a big band played salsa: brass, piano, conga drums, and a tenor voice that belonged, he told me, to Hector Lavoe. He offered to change the CD, and said he owns every kind of music, from Duke Ellington to Elvis and Johnny Cash. I told him I was happy to listen to Hector Lavoe. I'd never heard of him before.

Cookie wears her hair with feathered bangs and the ends turning in toward her chin, a style last popular around 1972. She's a radiology nurse at Montefiore. The lines around her mouth aren't happy lines, but they don't seem bitter, either. She served us sponge cake with almond syrup, and listened to our conversation as she brewed coffee and cleaned up.

Framed letters, photos, and certificates covered one wall, from waist height almost to the ceiling. I asked about that, and Cookie said over her shoulder, "He helped so many kids. They still call and check in."

Oscar's early life, I learned, followed a common pattern. After his father died, he started getting in trouble for throwing rocks at other kids—or, not rocks, but chunks of playground asphalt. After detention came suspension. Only one person in the school saw something in him worth saving. The assistant principal, a scary guy named Mr. Zajac, sat him down and said, "If I was you, I'd be screaming all day long—if they did that to my old man." Oscar cried in his office. "I couldn't stop. I was shaking like crazy. He let me cry as long as I had to."

Mr. Zajac gave him a set of dumbbells for his birthday and showed him how to use them. They played one-on-one basketball on the weekends. "All I ever wanted was to be like him. To find kids that were messed up and unmess them." He worked as a gym teacher for fifty years, and retired just this past June. He said he planned to keep talking to school groups about sports and mental health.

I explained that, like him, I had wanted to help families with problems, but I knew I didn't have the temperament for face-to-face counseling, so I've been helping indirectly for thirty years, administering Medicaid.

"Hey," he said, "you're in the fight, that's what counts."

I told him that I had just learned about his father's death, and the story haunted me. He said, "That's my only complaint in life. He went away when I was seven. I don't even have that many memories of him."

He said he wanted to show me what his father was like. I wasn't sure what that meant. "It's something I put together," he said, and opened a black laptop on the dinner table.

The slideshow began with a photo of a little boy in shorts and a button-down shirt, looking up admiringly at a bigger boy. "That's him with Uncle Willie. My dad's the little one." A grainy close-up of a class picture: no smile. Standing on a rooftop with his mother's hands on his shoulders, alongside a brick chimney. (Solid and stern, in a long, flowery skirt, this was the woman who wrote that letter to my father.) Sitting on a horse, scared but thrilled: "His uncle had a farm upstate." At the beach with his brother and cousins, smiling just a bit, the skinniest of them all. An official army portrait, hand-colored. In an army hospital, under a white sheet, grim. Returning home, in uniform, hugged by both parents at once. (In that one, you could just make out the scar: a short slash on the neck, lighter than the skin around it.) In satin boxing trunks, posing in a crouch. ("He took it up after the army, before I was born. He was a featherweight.") Kissing his wife-to-be in front of a sidewalk soda fountain. The wedding photo, with parents and siblings, every man with a mustache. At work in a dark custodian's uniform, up on a ladder, fixing a light fixture with a screwdriver. ("He could fix anything. See that clock? It stopped, so the school replaced it. He brought it home and took it apart, and it's been running ever since.") Pushing a baby carriage with Marquita clutching his arm, in front of Bohack, a supermarket whose name I hadn't heard since childhood. Showing little Oscar how to hold a baseball bat, on a sidewalk lined with parked 1950s cars. Feeding another baby a bottle while Oscar leaned against his shoulder. ("That's my sister, she's a Special Ed teacher.") Resting a hand proudly on the rounded hood of his first car. ("It was a '51 Packard. But my mom never learned to drive, so she sold it.") Dressed up to go out, German in a suit, Marquita in a long dress. ("That was their anniversary. Same year he got arrested.")

You can't see all the sides of a person's soul in snapshots, but German made a distinct impression. In almost every picture, his eyebrows rose like the two sides of a peaked roof. Even during the better times, he looked like something sharp and heavy was dangling over his head, just above the frame. What had happened to him? You had to wonder.

"He was gentle. He never lost his temper—except once, when some kid in the park punched me. He came storming over and slapped that kid's face, and I mean hard. He said, 'Don't come near my son again!' It scared me, seeing him that way."

Oscar had to remind me why I'd come. "You wanted to talk about the war, right? What they went through together."

I said I wanted to hear whatever he knew, but I couldn't share much, because my father never told stories about the war. I didn't want him to know that Dad had never mentioned his father.

Everything he said rang true, at first. "There were some bad apples in that platoon, but they had some great men too. When my papi got hit, Morris stopped the bleeding. He pressed on the wound with his bare hands, and then he fed my dad wound tablets to fight off an infection."

"Your father told you a lot."

"He didn't like talking about the war, but I kept bugging him. I'm glad I did too. If I waited one more year, I wouldn't of heard anything."

"Did he mention the bullying?"

"Yeah, he did. I wanted to hear more about this Morris guy, the one who helped him. He said there was this one soldier who stuttered. The jerks would push him around, but Morris went over and stopped it. I asked him if he helped, too, and he said, 'A couple times'—but they didn't like Puerto Ricans and he had to be careful."

He saw something in my face. "What?"

"Nothing. Just...I wanted my father to be more heroic too."

He gave me a funny look. "What are you talking about? Your pops was like Superman."

He told me how, when his father was at his weakest, mine had kept him from giving up by asking questions about his family. "Once he got to thinking about his parents, he knew what it would do to them if he didn't come home. That made him fight for his life."

"He must have lost a lot of blood," I said.

"No kidding. They had to give him a bunch of transfusions."

I imagined German slung over my father's shoulder, not knowing if he would live another hour. They were only nineteen.

"My dad got shot too. But he didn't tell me much about it."

"My papi said it felt like someone jabbed him in the leg. He didn't know he was shot until he felt the blood dripping down."

Cookie joined us at the table. He held her hand.

"When he came to our apartment that day, my mom thought it was the police. She told us to not make a sound. But then he called out, 'It's Morris Weintraub.'"

I said I was amazed that he remembered so much.

"There's a reason. Mr. Zajac told me to write down every memory I had of my father. He said, 'Any time you remember something else, add it to the list. Someday you'll be glad you took the time.'"

If German had lied to his son about being bullied in the army, he might also have lied to my father about trying to shoot the congressman. I couldn't imagine a way to ask the question that wouldn't offend Oscar. "I don't want you to think I'm disrespecting your father's memory, but there's something I need to know."

"Ask away."

"Your father said he had nothing to do with that shooting, and my father believed him. Is there any chance it wasn't true? Because—I'm just not clear on how they could convict him based only on a resemblance."

Oscar nodded, considering the question. I worried that his next words would be, *Get out of my house.*

"A couple of witnesses picked him out in a lineup. We spent years trying to prove he was innocent. My mom and my uncle kept going back to that street to look for the old lady with the dog. They found her, too, and she recognized my dad from his picture—but she couldn't swear she saw him that day in particular."

Long after his father died, though, they got an anonymous phone call. A man had been arrested for shooting a cop, and he fit the description of the guy who had tried to assassinate Adam Clayton Powell. The police didn't want to pursue it, but the family might want to hire someone to investigate. The caller wouldn't say who he was, but he gave them the suspect's name, Fernando Argueyes. Oscar thought the call must have come from a police detective.

At the library, Oscar learned that Argueyes had been convicted and sent to Matteawan, a hospital for the criminally insane. He took a train upstate by himself and tried to visit the inmate, claiming he was a friend of the family. But he was just a teenager and they wouldn't let him in.

Unwilling to give up, he wrote to the prison superintendent, who wrote back and promised to have a doctor question Argueyes. Oscar waited, and finally sent a follow-up letter, but the superintendent never replied.

"What do you think happened?"

"I think the word came from on high. *Shut the hell up. Act like these people don't exist, and hope to God they go away.*"

He contacted a reporter from the *World-Telegram*, who went to Matteawan and said he was Argueyes's brother-in-law. The reporter got in easily. Instead of asking Argueyes *if* he tried to kill Adam Clayton Powell, he asked *why*. The answer: "I already tell both doctors—because he wanted to put us to the bottom, under *los negros.*" *Us* meaning Puerto Ricans. "This creep was seriously wacko."

Oscar excused himself for a moment and came back with a three-ring binder. He flipped past some handwritten letters in sheet protectors and showed me a newspaper headline that read, *Falsely Accused, Wrongly Convicted, Senselessly Murdered.* The year was 1967. Under the headline were two photos: German in his army uniform and little Oscar between his parents.

I reached over and squeezed his arm. (My hand only made it halfway around.) Our fathers had told the truth. He'd proved it.

Based on their modest apartment, I assumed they had only gotten a small settlement, if any. He explained that he hadn't even wanted money, he just wanted them to admit what they had done—"but my mom was sick by then, she had ovarian cancer. So, yeah, we took the settlement, and after we paid off the medical bills we had enough left to go out to supper, me and my sister. In Chinatown."

He slipped a folded page out of its sheet protector and opened it carefully. "Take a look at that."

The full-page article included three pictures: the police sketch that led to German's arrest and two mug shots, one of German and one of Argueyes, who looked about fifteen years older, was bald, and had no mustache. In the police sketch, the shooter wore a dark, narrow-brimmed hat. The drawing looked more like German than Argueyes.

"Now I'll show you one more thing," Oscar said, and turned

to the back of the binder. The last sheet protector held a photocopy of the same three pictures, but someone had drawn a hat and mustache on the one of Argueyes. Now he was the one who matched the police sketch—perfectly.

"He wore a fake mustache that day," Oscar said. "All they really had in common was a scar on the neck."

I asked if he knew how his father had gotten that scar. He said it came from a fight when he was a kid, visiting his cousins in Florida. Some of the locals made fun of the way he spoke Spanish, because German had grown up in New York and had a different accent.

Outside, the sky had turned a luminous sea-blue. In a window across the street, a man was vacuuming in boxer shorts.

"You have a strong will," I said. "You kept fighting."

"My mami wanted to give up. My sister too. I felt like it was my mission."

I asked about the letters in the binder. What were those?

"He wrote to us every week from prison. I have some, my sister has the rest."

He tilted the binder toward me and let me turn the pages for myself. *I need new pictures so I know what you look like now... Make sure you read every night so you get good at it... Uncle Freddy said he would sign you up for Little League and you can practice with Bobby and Richie.*

The voice in the letters sounded intelligent. Responsible. Normal.

"You mentioned that your sister is a Special Ed teacher."

"Yeah, out of all the people I ever met, she's the only one I'd call a saint."

"It's interesting that you both ended up working with kids."

"That's because both of us got rescued in school. We both found grown-ups who cared. We were lucky."

Cookie asked if she could get me more coffee. I said I should probably start heading home.

"Wait," Oscar said. He bent his head, as if praying. "I just want to say how much it means to me that you came. That I can sit here with Morris's son. I never expected it."

Tears came to him more quickly than to me. But I wanted to keep up with him, to go where he was going, as much as I could.

"I have to tell you," I said, "I didn't think of my father the way you think of him. All we ever saw was a friendly guy who made people laugh."

His forehead wrinkled in perplexity.

"You have to understand, everything you admire about him, he kept secret from us."

"I guess he didn't want to brag. But he should have told you more, so you would know him. I wouldn't be here if not for him. I wouldn't have been born except for him carrying my pop on his back."

All I could do was nod. It would take time and solitude to absorb that.

We agreed to stay in touch. I couldn't remember the last time I met a man I liked as much.

As he led me to the door, I read a random sentence from one of the framed letters. *My professors are cool, but they give too much work.*

"You've accomplished a lot," I said. "Your father would be proud."

Cookie held her husband's arm the same way Marquita had held German's in front of Bohack. "That's the truth," she said.

Oscar gave me another bear hug at the door. No words, just a brother's embrace.

By saving German's life, my father had given him nine good years. Even at the best times, though, the persecuted look rarely left his face.

A question had been growing since Myriam read me the letter from German's mother. Had those assholes in the army done more than taunt him? Had the abuse been so humiliating that he could never tell anyone?

The highway lights went by, one after another, ticking off the seconds. My father may not have been around every time those men decided to entertain themselves with German. Imagining it, my head jerked to the side as if it were happening to me.

7

At my request, Charlotte mailed me the folder Dad had labeled *Platoon News*. Inside were updated mailing lists, postcards and letters, and a few editions of a one-page typed newsletter. The first mailing lists were handwritten; the last one was a computer printout dated 2005 and revised in pen. Those who had already died when he created this document had a notation after their names, a *D* and a date. Those who died afterwards had the same notation in the left margin. The writing wavered after his stroke. He must have used his left hand.

In the ten years since he'd printed the list, some of the addresses had changed, all to places further south. Only three names remained free of the grim pen notations: Pete Nielsen of Santa Barbara, Calif., Denny Lunceford of Shreveport, La., and Alvin Schwarz of Lebanon, Penna.

I wrote to them all by email, explaining that I hoped to find answers to a few questions about the war. Only Alvin wrote back. *I would be happy to oblige you.*

He preferred to meet in person rather than talk on the phone, because of his hearing loss. Before agreeing to drive to Pennsylvania, I asked if he remembered my father and German. *Who could forget?* he wrote.

We agreed to meet at a diner near his home the following Sunday afternoon. There would be few other customers then, and not much background noise.

Ellen gave me a deadly stare when I told her, reflected in the medicine chest mirror. It took me a moment to remember why: we had talked about driving to the Berkshires for the weekend. She had proposed the trip, and I'd jumped at the idea, the first sign of a thaw since Evan's visit. That I had forgotten must have been a slap in the face.

"I could write back and reschedule."

"No, go ahead. We can do it the weekend after. It doesn't matter."

I apologized. "I just need to ask him about a few things."

"You realize this could go on forever, right? There'll always be one more person to talk to."

This wasn't just about us. She's been desperate for distraction lately. One of her clients, convicted of insider trading, went to his niece's wedding recently and sat at a table with his co-defendants—i.e., his brothers-in-law—thereby violating the terms of his probation. Judge Shit-for-Brains, as she called him, sent this man to prison for a year. She blamed herself for mentioning the wedding in her report. She still takes these things to heart, and I respect her for that.

"Why don't you make a reservation at a B&B? I promise I won't forget."

She watched me in the mirror, inscrutable. "All right, I'll do that." Then she continued taking her makeup off, scrubbing one eye with one side of a wipe, the other with the other side, which left her raccoon-eyed. She pushed the door shut with her foot before finishing the job.

The diner was a haphazard conglomeration of brick, aluminum, and glass. The counter had round swivel stools, something I haven't seen in a while. A tired, pear-shaped woman in nursing scrubs was chatting gloomily with a customer. She asked me, "Just one?" and I explained that I was meeting someone, a man in his nineties.

A small drama played out on her face. Puppet lines formed around her mouth; her over-plucked eyebrows lowered like a barricade. She led me to a booth where an obese old man sat reading the menu.

His face was jowly and dotted with liver spots, moles, and skin tags. A pair of reading glasses sat low on his nose. A flesh-tone hearing aid sealed the ear that faced me.

"Alvin Schwarz?"

"Schwarzzz. There's no *T* and we're not in Germany."

(How many times has he said that, I wondered.)

We shook hands. The edge of the table pressed into his belly.

"They told me in 1965 I'd better lose weight or I'd drop dead. Meanwhile I've outlived four doctors."

His voice was sandy and faint, weaker than his words. His hair, a sparse fringe of silver, stood perpendicular to his scalp, a quarter-inch all around, except on top where a Band-Aid flattened it.

It was hard to look at him, and hard to look away. I reminded myself that an ugly face can happen to anyone; it has little to do with the soul. Ian's third-grade teacher, Mrs. Giorgakis, had boils and a nose like a lump of dough, but she was so kind that her students loved her, and so did their parents.

Small talk: he has lived in the area most of his life, except for four years working for Ernst & Whinney in Harrisburg; was married briefly (divorced, no children); owned a solo financial services business (stocks, bonds, taxes, insurance, estate planning); still does some day-trading; still drives ("Well, I wasn't going to walk"); doesn't go out at night any more. He never looked me in the eye, but he kept a close watch on my lips when I spoke.

The waitress seemed inexplicably hostile when she came back. Schwarz ordered the roast pork platter. I chose the turkey and bacon on whole wheat. She gave me a gruff "Mm-hm," which was more than she gave him. "Attitude problem," he said when she was gone.

I assumed she'd had some unhappy dealings with him in the past, perhaps a history of stingy tips. There *was* something off-putting about him, though. His repartee seemed cordial, but he never smiled.

"So what would you like to know?" he asked.

I explained that I'd heard some contradictory stories, and asked if he was willing to tell me what really happened during the war, to the extent he could remember, without sugar-coating.

"If you really want to hear it."

Before we began, he needed to mention a lakefront property

in the Poconos. A friend had passed away recently, and he told
the kids he would let them know if he ran across a potential
buyer. "It would make a fabulous summer home, or a perfect
place to retire. The family's trying to save the realtor's commis-
sion. You can understand that."

I told him I was sorry about his friend, but I'd never wanted
the headache of a summer home, and our apartment in Jersey
City was our retirement home. He showed me a snapshot of a
pond—"That's from the front porch"—and gave me his business card in case I reconsidered.

Instead of answering questions about German Rosario, I
suggested he start by sharing some memories of the army. He
misunderstood my purpose.

"This isn't elegant dining conversation, but since you
asked… The Germans used to set up little mines in wooden
boxes that our mine detectors couldn't find. Just enough TNT
to blow off your foot. They called them shoe mines. But that
was nothing. When they shelled us, you'd see people get blown
apart. Intestines hanging from the bushes like Christmas dec-
orations. Bodies on the hillside, burnt from head to toe. Guys
hit with so many bullets, there was nothing left of their faces.
Whoever found them usually threw up. The reports just said
'KIA.' The families never knew. Lucky them."

He said all of this without perceptible emotion. I apologized
for asking him to dredge up these things, and he said, "Not
at all. And by the way, one of the worst smells in the world is
blood under a hot sun."

I asked if he understood the part their platoon had played in
the war, because I didn't. He said, "It's not complicated. We had
to push the Germans north, out of Italy. But they had other
ideas."

I asked what he remembered about my father. Before answering, he went back to the property in the Poconos. "Let me
give you this, to show your wife. She may want to come out and
take a look." He handed me a two-page real estate listing with
photos of a small green cabin. It looked like a rest room in a
state park. The pond came perilously close to the front steps.

I folded the page and slipped it into my shirt pocket. "All right, but I can tell you now, we're not your best bet."

Was that what turned him into an enemy? He showed nothing, he seemed placid, but the conversation darkened after that.

"I was with your father the first time he shot a Kraut. I congratulated him on losing his virginity. He didn't want to take a souvenir, so I did it for him. Nothing barbaric, just a collar patch."

"I think I found it in his belongings."

"Good, he kept it. I'm glad. By the way, here's something most civilians don't know: after you watch a buddy or two die, you enjoy killing the enemy."

He was drifting into territory I preferred not to explore, not because I couldn't bear it, but because I doubted that his insights applied to my father. "I also found what looks like a German pistol, and some bullets. Do you think those were souvenirs too?"

"What else would they be? After a battle, you'd go collecting. Everybody did it."

I asked what he could tell me about German Rosario.

He shook his head. The wattle under his chin swung like a sail. "I don't know what he was doing in our platoon. They had a separate regiment for PRs."

That gave me a clearer idea of the person I was sitting with. "So, he didn't fit in?"

"He was a runt. His pack weighed more than he did. And he was scared shitless all the time. Not to mince words."

I asked if he thought the bullying had more to do with his size or the fact that he was Puerto Rican.

"Both. But I wouldn't call it bullying. More like hazing."

Could he give me examples?

The waitress brought our food as he told his stories. His plate—sliced meat in gravy, mashed potatoes, corn, sauerkraut, and a roll—banged loudly against the old Formica tabletop. He didn't pause, and she didn't apologize.

"Most of it was verbal. People called him a spy, because of his name. Harmless teasing, nothing vicious. One time (this was hilarious) they found a syringe and injected Ben-Gay into his toothpaste. But he earned it. He couldn't pull his weight."

Schwarz tore his roll in two, spread a pat of butter on each half, and took his time chewing.

"Who hazed him, mainly? Who put the Ben-Gay in his toothpaste?"

"That would be Donaldson and Hiller. They were from down South. Tall and short, quiet and loud. They went together like Mutt and Jeff."

My father had told me so little. Aside from the IQ test and peeing blood when he got shot, the only army story I knew was how he'd misheard his drill sergeant's name. It was *Soja*, but Dad thought he'd said, *Soldier.* "Sergeant Soldier." Such a child-like mistake.

Beneath the other questions, the darkest one waited. I found it hard to speak the words. "You don't think it ever got to the point… You don't think German got raped?"

He said matter of factly, "Not as far as I know."

I explained that German's mother had sent my father a letter after the war. She seemed to believe he had protected German from abuse. "Do you remember anything like that?"

His face showed nothing: not concentration, not annoyance. "Maybe. Once or twice."

"What happened?"

He cut a pork slice methodically into quadrants. Gravy spilled over the edge of the plate.

"I know it was a long time ago," I said.

"Sorry to disappoint you, but all your papa did was say a few words. 'Come on, guys, knock it off.' That sort of thing. He wasn't the type to throw a punch."

I must have made a face—*Of course he wasn't*—and he may have misinterpreted it. That would explain the change in his tone.

"You told me not to sugar-coat it. Your father wasn't that different from his pal. They were two little guys. Not exactly tough."

The insult surprised me. I asked if he knew that my father

had stayed with German when he got shot, and most likely saved his life.

Gravy dripped from his meat as he brought it to his lips. "I don't like to say these things, but you're on a hunt for the truth, right? You might as well know. Your father talked a lot. That's how he dealt with the fear. It was annoying to some people. When Rosario got hit, we were advancing, with machine guns unloading on us. I don't think Morris minded staying behind. He didn't need to hold Rosario's hand, a medic could have taken care of him. They were talking about a court-martial, supposedly. But the lieutenant got killed before he wrote up the papers. Your daddy lucked out."

At first I assumed that Schwarz was just a son-of-a-bitch who, for mysterious reasons, had decided to deface my father's memory, to poison my idea of him. I wanted to punch him—a feeling I haven't had since childhood. But I didn't want to hide from the facts, if these were the facts. It *might* have happened the way he said.

I thought of my father in the kitchen after midnight, eating his solitary bowl of cereal—bare-chested, and so hairy that I could never find the scars where the bullets went in. I had often wondered what those scars looked like, but never asked him to show me, for fear he would get angry.

"It brings me no joy to tell you this, but when I read about the prison thing, I had to wonder. What went on between those two? I'm not judging, but you have to ask the question. Why was he always protecting his little friend?"

Okay, so Schwarz wanted to get inside my head and do damage. I would put the odds that my father and German had some sort of homosexual relationship at about one in fifty thousand—but I couldn't deny that it was possible. *Anything* is possible.

The world has changed since Schwarz's time. If it happened, I wouldn't think less of Dad. But Schwarz meant it as a slur. He wanted me to be horrified: *Was my old man a homo?*

The only other customer in the place was a man in his thirties, in jeans with mud at the ankles and a black T-shirt.

Our waitress shook her head as she talked to him—grousing, it seemed—and coughed into her shoulder.

"People aren't that admirable, deep down," Schwarz said. "You learn that pretty fast in the army. Once you get to know them, nobody's a hero."

I had one more question, but I hesitated, because he might answer with a lie that I wouldn't be able to see through. There was no one else to ask, though.

I took the photo of my father and Silvia from my shirt pocket. "Do you have any idea who the girl is?"

She looked very young, unable to hide her feelings. If he said, *She was a whore,* I wouldn't believe him.

"No clue. We all met girls. Sometimes their mothers pushed them on us. They were hungry; some of them just wanted our C-rations. Some were more ambitious. A lot of promises got made."

This sounded true in general, but I doubted that my father had lied to get Silvia into bed. I couldn't imagine it. She did seem anxious to stay with him, though.

"Did you do that? Promise to marry someone?"

He filled his fork with sauerkraut and paused, considering the question.

"When you just survived a war, and you see the things we saw—and then you meet a young girl who thinks you're a big shot… But you never fought in a war, correct?"

"That's right."

"You'd understand if you had. You'll promise her anything she asks for."

Maybe.

"We wanted something and they wanted something. It was a negotiation."

(Was it possible that the German soldier hadn't taken that ring? Maybe he'd put it in his pocket when he went to see Silvia, and lost it.)

"I'll tell you something about those girls. They knew a lot. They were good Catholic virgins—they had all sorts of tricks."

Reaching for my ice tea, I knocked over the little pitcher of maple syrup. Not much leaked out, but wiping it spread the syrup around. I had to dip a few napkins in my water glass to clean the mess.

Schwarz observed all this impassively. "By the way," he said, "I wouldn't be surprised if you had a half brother or sister over there."

I'd had the same thought myself, the night I found Silvia's picture. It made me extremely uncomfortable: somewhere in Italy, a man might be going about his business, a man who looked like Dad, or like me, someone who had grown up poor and bitter—possibly a criminal. Or a woman who wondered why her father never cared enough to look for her.

Each of Schwarz's eyelids had skin tags among the lashes, small excrescences like grains of sand. He pretended to be an objective truth-teller, but his words were a stream of quiet malice. They held the power to sow confusion and doubt. It seemed important to resist.

"Why would he have been in Rome, anyway? I thought your company fought near Florence."

"They let some of us tour Italy before we went home. This was after V-E Day—which we called V-D Day, because that's what happens when you let thousands of GIs loose in cities full of prostitutes."

I wanted to trap Schwarz, to trick him into admitting that he was twisting the truth. But I couldn't see a way to phrase the question.

"It seems like you might have a grudge against my father," I said. "Do you?"

If I'd caught him, neither his face nor his voice gave him away. "I don't know what you're talking about."

I had no evidence, but my suspicions had already hardened into a firm belief. I wanted him to know that I saw what he was doing. And so I stared him down.

There was still some corn on his plate, but he set down his fork. His hand trembled. "You can believe what you want to believe. You're the one who asked the questions."

"I just want to know why everything you say is an insult."

He shook his head dismissively, as if I were a lunatic. Like a giant bug, he inspired an urge to crush him—along with a dread of contact.

"Is it possible that you're one of the people my father protected German from?"

He looked at me flatly. "Time for me to take off," he said.

He used a dark wooden cane, which I hadn't noticed. He made no offer to pay for his meal. As he walked away, he propped the cane at an angle to his hip, like a flimsy buttress. Each step began with a jerk, as if the ball-end of his thigh bone were popping out of its socket.

(Did I really imagine kicking the cane away? Yes, but only later. A malign fantasy.)

The waitress wandered over and growled, "Anything else?"

"I don't know that guy, but you seem to. What's his story?"

She cast her eyes toward the kitchen. "I don't tell tales."

"He just tried to sell me a load of BS about my father. They were in the army together. I wanted to spit at him."

That earned me some guarded sympathy. "I'll say this much: I'd put rat poison in his food if I had any."

We became allies. "I need to know if I should believe any of the things he said. Is the reason you don't like him that he's a liar?"

"Put it this way. If he says, Good morning, don't believe it."

It didn't take much coaxing to pry her grievance out of her.

"A long time ago, he talked a lot of people into buying some stock he swore would go way up, fast. Some medical equipment company. He had everybody convinced they'd make a fortune. Well, that stock dropped like a rock. People wanted to sell before they lost even more, but he quit answering his phone."

Had she lost money?

"I never had any to lose. But my sister did, and my uncle, and some friends."

Knowing he had screwed his neighbors reassured me somehow. But it didn't explain why he would lie to me. There was no profit in it for him.

"He said he'd been married for a while. Did you know his wife?"

"That was before my time. My mom said she lasted about two months and then ran."

I left her a generous tip. When I went to pay, I found her at the register.

"I don't know how he has the nerve to show his face," she said. "He must think we've forgotten. We won't ever forget."

I had his address. Before driving back, I took a five-minute detour.

The outside of his home revealed nothing. A modest brick ranch house with a freshly mowed lawn, its only distinguishing feature was a newly planted cherry tree in front. He wasn't impoverished, apparently: he could afford to pay a landscaper. Unlike his neighbors, he didn't fly a flag.

I don't want to delude myself. As unreliable as Schwarz may be, his version of history would explain why Dad never talked about the war.

To believe him, though—even in part, even for a moment— would be to betray my father. Maybe Dad's personality repelled Schwarz, as a cross repels a vampire.

Silvia, though.

Imagine it: the bastard child of an American soldier, fathered by my father. The life that person would have lived.

I switched on the radio and searched for something to take me away from Schwarz and his stories. On the local NPR station, Robert Siegel said that ISIS had destroyed an ancient temple in Palmyra, Syria. The militants had tortured and beheaded the retired director of antiquities there, an eighty-one-year-old man.

I searched for a different station, and found Bruce Springsteen singing "Thunder Road." Even at high volume, the song couldn't obliterate the image of the severed head.

We live in Schwarz's world, not my father's. The evidence is hard to deny.

8

A lie is such an effective poison. Those who want to believe it will instantly accept it as true. Those who idolize the target of the smear will wonder and worry, because we know that most of us are capable of almost anything. My father may have stayed with German because he didn't want to get shot at. He may have narrowly escaped a court-martial. Or Schwarz may have made those things up because he's a hateful son of a bitch.

The *Platoon News* mailing lists don't include anyone named Donaldson or Hiller. Either Dad left them out because he refused to have anything to do with them, or Schwarz disguised their names for reasons of his own.

More mysteries.

A story in the *Times* about a terrorist's trial included an excerpt from the court transcript in which the defendant and the judge exchanged fiery harangues. After I put the paper down, I realized that a record of my father's trial may still exist in an archive somewhere. If I can put my hands on it, I thought, I may find the answers to many questions.

A helpful clerk at New York State Supreme Court looked it up. "There is no transcript," he told me. It sat in a warehouse for decades, and burned in a fire a few months ago, along with many years' worth of records. The timing couldn't have been more frustrating.

Having gotten my hopes up, I wasn't ready to let go. The lawyer who defended my father might still be alive. People live past a hundred all the time.

I found his name in one of my father's newspaper clippings. A quick search turned up an article from eight years ago, about two neighbors and the leopard that came between them.

Neighbor One owned a pet shop and kept a leopard cub in an enclosure in his yard, but the cat got out one day and ate a dachshund belonging to Neighbor Two, a retired lawyer. There was more—about their day in court, their ongoing feud, etc.— but all I needed was the location: Imperial Avenue in Westport, Connecticut.

The phone was in my hand, the area code already dialed. *Why am I doing this?* I asked myself. *What's the point?* It was time to let go. I had already done all that could be expected of a dutiful son.

I knew Ellen would heartily approve if I put the phone down and ended my search. But I dialed the lawyer's number anyway.

Wonder of wonders: Martin Scofield had just gotten out of Brooklyn Law School when he defended my father. He remembered the case, and invited me to visit.

The following weekend, Ellen and I stayed two nights at a B&B in Lenox, Massachusetts. We poked around in art galleries and the Norman Rockwell Museum, walked along the Housatonic River, climbed Monument Mountain, and ate at a funky restaurant called the Gypsy Joynt. It was idyllic, but no good.

Her discontent filled the car like a bad smell on the way up. By the time we reached the George Washington Bridge, I couldn't stand it. I said, "Are you still angry about Evan, or is something else going on?"

Her posture changes when she's about to state a grievance. The small childhood scar at the bottom of her chin nearly touched the malachite teardrop of her necklace.

"Some of it's work," she said. She explained that she's thinking about changing careers. She's tired of her clients, tired of her supervisors, tired of the disappointments and the paperwork. She'd like to try something new. Garden design is one possibility. Everyone used to admire our yard, and she misses playing around with new plantings. She could start as an apprentice to Doris Pezzullo.

I pointed out that she would probably need some kind of

certification if she wanted to go out on her own. She said she had already looked into a few programs.

There was an obvious problem with her plan. "But by the time you finish the training and the apprenticeship, you'll be old enough to retire."

She turned her face to the window.

I tried to retract what I'd said. "On the other hand, if you work for yourself, you don't have to retire."

"It's not just work," she said. "Something has to change. My life is slipping away and I'm just watching it go."

I was afraid to ask what she meant. I wasn't sure how drastic a change she had in mind.

"Nothing to say?"

"I guess you should explain."

So she did. For the next twenty minutes, she let me have it: how I've imposed my way of maintaining the peace, keeping everything calm and reasonable, no matter what... how sometimes she wants to shout but stops herself because she knows I'll give her the look that means, *You're acting hysterical.* If we're to go on, she said, she'll need something new. "If I decide to say, 'Fuck it, I'm changing careers,' you'll have to support that, not try to talk me out of it."

I told her I understood, and *would* support it. "I'll help in any way I can."

She didn't acknowledge that, and didn't speak again until she asked for a rest stop at the Connecticut border.

At dinner, we found ourselves looking up at the many colorful flags and strings of lights. A waitress with hair the color of a goldfish joked with the parents of three redheaded kids: "So I guess you want the special discount." I liked that, and thought Ellen would too, but she was reading her menu, not ready to let go of her discontent. The corners of her mouth turned down.

"I've been thinking about what you said on the way up," I told her. "I think garden design makes a lot of sense for you."

"Mm-hm."

"And as far as the rest of it: I'm willing to bend."

"That's good."

She said it ironically, as if, in a test of generosity, I'd volunteered a nickel. Anger ignited in me, as it had the night of
the orange. But fear infected the anger and stole its force. I
saw myself coming home after work and finding her gone, her
closet and dresser empty. It made me light-headed.

That was last Saturday, a week ago. Not much has changed
since then. She hasn't visited my side of the bed, but she hasn't
disappeared, either.

I asked if she would object to my driving up to Connecticut
to interview my father's lawyer. She said, "Why should I?"

My phone directed me over the Hudson and across Westchester,
to a ranch house with three chimneys and an attached two-car
garage, overlooking the Saugatuck River. A top-heavy woman
welcomed me at the door in a leather mini-skirt and a pearly silk
blouse, unbuttoned to the center of her bra. She looked about
forty and wore her hair in a bob, two sharp hooks cutting in at
her cheeks. "You had good drive?" she asked, her accent thick
and Russian. Oddly, she seemed glad to see me.

The house smelled of mildew, cigar smoke, mandarin oranges, and, faintly, feces. Light gray carpeting covered the hallway
and every room but the kitchen; the darker nap showed the
recent path of a vacuum cleaner. In the dining room, a dozen
amber vials clustered in the center of a round table. Framed
photos in the hall showed my host and his family in Africa,
India, and Alaska, many decades ago.

In the living room, a frail, yellowish man on a three-wheeled
scooter was reading the *Wall Street Journal* on a gigantic monitor,
the type magnified to half an inch. A caddy on the back of the
scooter's seat held a slender oxygen tank.

"Martin."

He turned and snapped, "What, Natalie?" Seeing me, he
shifted gears. "Mr. Weintraub, I presume. Welcome!"

The top of his head gleamed as if polished. His lips were
bluish purple. The upper lid of one eye was swollen, puffy.

Although he kept an oxygen tube draped over his shoulder, a cigar stub stood vertically in an ashtray, still giving off smoke.

He maneuvered the scooter around the couch and shook my hand. His skin was soft and very cold. Once I settled myself in the corner of the couch, he pulled up at a right angle to the coffee table so we could talk without staring straight at each other. "Can we offer you a drink? I stock beers of all nations." I asked if he had a German Weissbier, and Natalie said, "I look."

He has survived three kinds of cancer—colon, prostate, and lymphoma—but can't beat the emphysema. (That's the cause of the blue lips, he said, and also the blue fingertips, which I hadn't noticed.) He takes so many pills, he can't remember what they're all for. His eye is swollen because they repaired the lens two weeks ago. He has gone back to eating red meat and ice cream, and smokes a couple cigars a week—giving God the finger, he said.

Although his furnishings signaled prosperity and status far greater than my father's (grand piano, giant explorer's globe) his medical condition narrowed the gap between them. Watching him scoot around the room with his oxygen canister reminded me of the proverb: *After the game, the king and the pawn go in the same box.*

A painted portrait of his late dachshund hung over the fireplace. *Fritzi,* a small brass nameplate said. The mantel was crowded with pictures of Scofield's wife, children, grandchildren, and great-grandchildren. A yahrzeit candle burned amid the photos—for his daughter, he explained.

"You're Jewish?"

"I changed my name after law school. 'Marvin Shapiro' lacked that certain *je ne sais quois.*"

I asked what happened to the leopard in the end. His gray eyes twinkled. "He had to give it to a zoo. He hasn't spoken to me since. A blessing."

He seemed to be a talker by nature, a storyteller, but the emphysema forced him to parcel out phrases between panting breaths.

Natalie returned with a silver tray the size of an LP. It held an open bottle of Erdinger, a tall, chilled glass, and a Manhattan for my host.

I asked Scofield how my parents had found him. He said, "My cousin married your father's sister."

It took me a moment to work that out. Uncle Irv! Suddenly this decrepit stranger turned into something else entirely: family. It's funny how that works.

I said he seemed to have done very well for himself. He replied that he owed everything to the GI Bill and to the celebrities he'd represented in DWI cases. ("Anyone I'd know?" "Probably not. Old character actors, mostly. Ever hear of Cecil Richardson? J.J. O'Brien? Emil Weiss?")

My call had set loose a flood of memories, he said. For years after the trial, my father's sentence had gnawed at him. "Three years out of a long and otherwise happy life, that's not a lot, right? But it changes everything. It becomes the biggest fact about you. *My fellow man locked me up in prison.* It leaves a bitter taste."

This sounded true in general, but I doubted that it applied to my father. "He was the least bitter man I've ever known."

"He may have been good at hiding things."

Oof, as my sons used to say.

I asked what kind of impression my father had made on him. He nodded: a faint tremor. "In a way, he was like a child. He had a naïve faith in the system. He assumed the authorities would understand why he did what he did. I told him his confidence was excessive, but he wouldn't listen. I said he should plead guilty and ask for leniency—since, after all, he did what they charged him with. But he wouldn't listen, and I didn't have decades of experience to back me up. He figured, How can it be a crime to help an innocent man? He didn't understand what he was up against. Not until the trial got under way."

Panting followed each of those sentences. When the story was done, he fitted the cannula to his nostrils and turned to open the valve on the oxygen tank.

"I liked your father," he said. "He was a nice guy, a loyal friend. I blamed myself for what happened—I shouldn't have let him talk me into going to trial. If he'd taken a plea right off the bat, he would have served a year at most."

I could see my father's side, though. Why volunteer for a year in prison if you're sure a jury will acquit you? "But he didn't think he'd done anything wrong."

"Unfortunately, it's not always about right and wrong. That's what he couldn't accept."

"You didn't think the jury would sympathize?"

His voice climbed in pitch. "I only agreed to go to trial because he was the most sympathetic defendant you could ask for. A guy who runs to help his buddy instinctively! And they both had Purple Hearts! The prosecutor had to prove intent to violate the law—but that was never his intent. I had my summation ready before jury selection: *We all know this man isn't a criminal. It's up to you to do what's right.*"

I asked about my father's statement at sentencing, the one that had offended the judge.

He sighed theatrically. "I saw the hole he was digging for himself. I tried to interrupt him, but he wouldn't shut up. By the way, I've always wondered if someone put pressure on the judge. Your father never should have gotten that much time. But the whole world was watching."

By then Scofield looked ghostly, worn out, and impatient with the need to replenish his breath. While he rested, I explained that I had a couple of specific questions to ask. I doubted my father would have mentioned these things, and even if he had, it was unlikely Scofield would remember, but I had no one else to ask. "I'm trying to understand why, during the war, he stayed with Rosario instead of letting a medic take care of him. And is it true that he almost got court-martialed?"

Scofield held up a finger. *Wait.* He closed his eyes and inhaled deeply from the tube.

"I don't remember if he talked about that. But the medics had a lot on their hands. Maybe his friend wouldn't be getting help for a while."

Good enough, I thought. That's what I'll believe.

"You can look through the file if you'd like. It might fill in some blanks."

I don't think hearts actually stop at moments like this, but they seem to. There's a pause, and the next thump comes with double the force.

"You kept the file?"

"I thought I'd write a memoir about my most colorful cases, like Louis Nizer. But I never had the time. Now I have the time, but not the energy."

I asked if the file included a transcript of the trial.

"No, but you can piece together a lot from what's there."

I would have driven any number of hours to see that file. "Where is it stored?" I asked.

He chuckled and jerked his thumb toward the wall, like a hitchhiker. "In my office."

He called for Natalie and led us to the next room. With its old IBM computer, its sagging shelves full of law books, and its bulky fax machine, the office looked like the set of a play that took place in 1985.

He had run out of wall space and stacked a pair of tan two-drawer file cabinets atop the putty gray four-drawer cabinets. My father's file was in one of the top drawers, and he sent Natalie up on a stepladder to retrieve it. Once she reached the third step, Scofield had to look up to see the hem of her skirt. Her slender legs, in black pantyhose, seemed mismatched with her sturdy torso. Scofield placidly enjoyed the view; he glanced at me, raising his eyebrows a little. Ellen would have called him disgusting, but I didn't begrudge him this small pleasure.

She turned to ask, "Weintraub, Morris?" and caught us watching. My face may have reddened. "That's the one," Scofield said. She seemed amused, not offended.

A sturdy oak table in the center of the room served as a desk. Natalie carried in a high-back chair upholstered in bone white corduroy from the dining room.

"Stay as long as you like," the lawyer said. "Shout if you need anything. It's time for my exercise."

He rode the scooter out of the room, a rising whir. "Please

call to me if you want something," Natalie said. She gave me a little smile and followed him out.

Three poster-size photos in simple black frames faced me: reddish sand dunes at sunset, shallow water rushing over large round stones, and pine needles partially covered by melting snow. I imagined Scofield at Staples many years ago, furnishing his home office, hurrying up and down the aisles because he didn't have time for this nonsense.

The file was red-brown, the expanding kind, familiar from the summer when I worked in the mailroom of Dave's father's law firm. A matching cloth ribbon served as a closure; the knot in the bow had flattened over time. Inside I found an arrest report, photocopied white on black; a pink carbon copy of a detective's report; a few legal documents, all with the standard caption box, THE PEOPLE OF THE STATE OF NEW YORK against MORRIS WEINTRAUB, Defendant; typed notes for an opening statement; typed questions for the cross-examination of the cops who had arrested my father; a one-page memo to the file; and a yellow legal pad with several sheets of scrawled notes.

Above the top line of the legal pad, a neat heading said, *Morris Weintraub interview, 3-6-54.* After that, Scofield's handwriting became indecipherable. It resembled the wire from a spiral notebook, stretched lengthwise: a series of loops and zigzags, each letter reaching only a third of the way to the ruled line above it. I couldn't make out a word.

The legal documents began simply enough. *The defendant, in the County of Queens, City of New York, on or about March 4, 1954, knowingly and unlawfully harbored in his apartment...* Within a few lines, though, I was stupefied. The arrest report gave his height, weight, and hair color. The detective's report summarized my father's responses to questioning in one single-spaced page of bureaucratic cop-talk. *Suspect states he has full confidence in his friend's innocence of the charge.* In a memo to the file, Scofield wrote, *Client indicates he now wants to plead guilty, as I strongly advised before trial. In conversation, prosecutor agreed to recommend a lessened sentence despite inconvenience to the court.*

Returning to the interview notes, I made some educated guesses and slowly learned to decode the scrawl. When I reached the end, I called for Natalie and asked if I could borrow the notes and make copies. She asked Scofield, and he assigned her to copy the pages on his printer.

Scofield wrote the notes in his homemade shorthand, omitting many letters and words. For the most part, they included only my father's responses, not the questions.

—was at work @ p.o. whn he saw police sktch in ppr—lookd like GR—knew hm in army, Italy—neck scar same—thght: did he snap?

My eyes soon adapted, and supplied the missing letters.

—got # from Operator—phoned—no answer

—thought: he's in trouble—either way, innocent or guilty, he needs help

—left work, "sick"—called home for German's address, took subway to Bronx

[you thought you could help? how?]

—can't say—figured German would need lawyer, might not be thinking straight—"type of guy bad things happen to" [a shlimazel? "yeah, a Spanish shlimazel"]

As I got better at interpreting the almost Arabic script, I could hear my father's voice, far off and faint but distinctively *him*: not even thirty, sitting in a young lawyer's office, eagerly answering questions, supplying Uncle Irv's cousin with all the facts he would need. I wanted to warn him, to shield him from the calamity he didn't see coming—to shake him and make him understand.

[you were close friends in army?]

—not really—barely spoke to him—but "a decent guy"—small, nervous, kept to self

—bullied—they'd bump him, he'd land in mud (so much rain and mud, trucks couldn't get through, they delivered supplies by mule)

—Morris spoke up, told the others, "Someday you'll need him & he'll remember this"—"F you, Weintraub"

—Fred comes over—big guy, M's pal—"Leave him alone or deal with me"

—more incidents—2 men hold German down while 3rd pisses on face— brawl

—Morris & Fred line up support of platoon—bullying ends —but fear of retaliation

—German shot—medic also down—Morris went to him —"an automatic thing, couldn't just let him bleed to death" — gave 1st aid—"I didn't know what I was doing, tried to remember what they showed us"—stayed with him—thought German would die, but tried to instill hope—gave him rosary from nuns

[Nuns? ask later]

Rosario, rosaries. I wonder if they ever had that conversation. *Hey, you'll never guess what I do for a living.*

—German asked him to hear his confession

—long story: visit to Florida, fight with local kids—they caught his big brother alone, threw rocks at him—German saw, hid, afraid—brother hit on side of head, unconscious, went to hospital—no one knew German was there—lifelong guilt

— "how old were you?"— "6 or 7" — "Think of a kid, 6 or 7— would you expect him to fight off a mob of big kids with rocks?"—didn't help

But it was a good try, Dad.

—later on, same trip, German fought with same kids himself—hurt one, got cut on neck

The next passage was densely scribbled. Scofield must have gone back over his notes and inserted all the details he could remember.

—got to know German pretty well that day. "He wanted me to give messages to his parents and brother. I told him he could still pull through if he didn't give up. He said it was out of our hands. He was so calm. I respected him."

I never heard my father speak as seriously and straightforwardly as this. I wish I could have been there.

—waited for dark—felt bad, because German could have

died waiting—but the enemy still had the hill, they'd get shot if seen

—no contact after war, just holiday cards

[Back to the incident: you saw newspapers with the police sketch—knew you could get in trouble. Why did you go to him?]

—(thinking…) "I hoped he was innocent. Didn't want to see his life ruined because they couldn't tell the difference between one Puerto Rican and another. He had a hard enough time in the army."

—admits he got scared on the way to German's apartment — thought about turning around—but kept going

[you understood you were breaking the law? "wasn't sure about that." You knew there might be consequences, though. "I figured I could explain. I just wanted to help."]

—at German's door, no answer—called out, "It's Morris Weintraub"

— door opens—wife trembling uncontrollably

—German in hiding—school principal showed him the paper, advised him to go straight to police & explain—but he thought they'd lock him up forever—called wife, hid in park, then back to school after dark

—he would never hurt anyone, wife said

—the plan: hide him temporarily, find a lawyer

—wife gave Morris spare key to school

—he walked there—on the way, called home, said friend had small problem, might stay with them overnight

My mother must have questioned that. *What friend? What kind of problem? Why are you the one who has to help him?* I hadn't heard that voice in many years, but I could hear it again, clearly.

—dark inside school—had cigarette lighter but afraid to be seen through classroom windows—waited for eyes to adjust (light from Exit signs)—walked corridors calling German's name—no sign of him

—went around second time, knocking on doors, saying his own name

—finally an answer—"Okay"

—supply closet in gym, with basketballs, etc.—no windows —let Morris in, locked door again

—reunion by cigarette lighter—shook hands—forgot how scrawny German was

—he ate food his wife sent: apple, cold fried chicken in foil

—"you didn't do it, did you?"—"are you crazy?"—"maybe they'll catch the real guy"

—German shaking head, hopeless, upset—if Morris found him, cops will, too

[was he happy to see you again? "too panicked to think about that"]

—"Where were you when it happened? Can someone testify?"

—newspaper says shots fired at 1:20 the day before—lunch hour—"so who saw you?" "nobody"—he goes for long walks at lunch, stands looking out at the Sound, reads *Racing Form*— no one around, except old lady walking big black poodle—he sees her sometimes, nods hello so she won't be afraid—maybe they could find her

—new plan: 1. get lawyer, 2. find lady—but 1st, take him back to Queens—"no one will look for you there"

—German afraid of being spotted on the way—"they just want someone to blame, doesn't matter who"

Events proved him right, but his attitude bothers me: *The whole world is against me, there's no hope.* My father had more patience than I do.

—Morris reassures—"tomorrow we'll drive up there, park on street & wait for her—everything will be fine, you'll see"

How many times had he said that when I was growing up? If one of us had a problem—a test on math we didn't understand, an argument with a friend—those were the words he used, always: *Everything will turn out fine.* I hated hearing it. *No, it won't,* I wanted to scream, and sometimes did.

I touched the page, the wiggling line of ink. He's here, I thought.

—they disguised German for subway. Morris had brought shopping bag with Brylcream, comb, wife's makeup, razor, shaving cream, a jacket—police sketch showed a mustache, hat, & neck scar—so German shaved off mustache in teacher's bathroom, combed hair, covered scar w/ makeup (not perfect match but less noticeable than scar)

[omit at trial—sounds devious]

I disagreed. To me, he sounded smart. I wouldn't have guessed he could plan so cleverly.

—on subway, talked to German about Dodgers, spring training—trying to sound like 2 normal guys—German couldn't talk, kept watching others on train

—at home wife complained about lateness—she's high-strung, impatient, gets upset at little things

—he explained German's situation—wife pulled him into bedroom, blew up, "I don't want him here!"—wouldn't calm down

I could see her. When she got agitated like that, her face and throat flushed. It happened on our trip to Niagara Falls, when we couldn't find a motel with a vacancy. And when she saw Paul playing on the railroad tracks at the end of our street in Johnson City.

—kids 6 & 2, wife expecting 3rd—luckily, bought a TV recently, let them watch *Ozzie & Harriet*.

Remember, though: there was another baby, stillborn, who came before Paul. Mom might have been a different person if that baby had lived.

(Holly would have been the third child. No need for another. I wouldn't exist.)

—uncomfortable dinner—kids scared of German—he never smiled

—German's uncle had a lawyer (crooks robbed his store, he hit them with a bat)—they called uncle, got the lawyer's #— no answer

—Morris: We need people who can tell the cops you're peaceful, not violent, don't even own a gun. Who could testify?

—but German *does* own gun—got it because of break-ins in his building—never used it

Oy. Dad must have felt like he was dragging boulders in a sack.

—just after 11, police knocked—loud

—in bed—wife grabbed his arm

—he offered to hide German in closet, behind wife's dresses —no, wouldn't do it

—German shaking with fear—"Calm down, don't act like this"—couldn't stop

—opened door, apologized for delay—"we were sleeping"

—handcuffed fast—both of them—wife crying (kids didn't wake up, fortunately)

—a neighbor called, said Morris came home with a guy— could be the one

—he knows who it was: Samberg, an accountant, "fussy like an old woman"—was going out when they came in

—Morris explained—"we have to find that witness, if you lock him up, how can he prove where he was?"—younger cop seemed to sympathize, older one didn't

—"at least let *me* go look for her"

—young cop unsure—old cop said, "you're gonna risk your job for a spic?"

—one last try: "he's in trouble for something he didn't do— what if we went to that street right now and knocked on doors? maybe we can find his witness."

I'd never seen this side of him. The only time I ever saw him interact with a cop was when he got stopped for speeding upstate. He was nervous and deferential. I hated it.

—old cop told him to shut up

—they almost arrested wife too, but Morris argued: "she didn't even want him in the house!"

—they questioned her—kids asleep, she couldn't leave them there alone—they let her stay—warned her not to disappear or she could lose custody

It's a miracle she didn't faint. Maybe she did.

—taken to Manhattan precinct—answered every question
—"I had nothing to hide"—confident in system.

[over-confident—but don't scare him.]

[You had to know you'd be on the wrong side of the law if
you hid him. I'll ask again: why take the risk? "I thought I could
help him. I pushed the fear to the side of my mind."]

—"can you do anything for German? at least make sure he
has a decent lawyer"

["I'll see who's representing him"—wanted to say, you
should worry about yourself.]

In the middle frame, in front of me, a film of clear water rushed
over the round stones. One was gray, one brown, one tan with
black specks. Those stones have been lying in that riverbed for
thousands of years, I thought. They must still be there: the river
must still be flowing over them. Some things last, simple and
beautiful.

Finally, I knew my father. He was the same man I'd known
all my life. Nobler than I realized, and smarter. Naïve in some
ways, but clever. Not larger than life: exactly life-size. He deserved my admiration, and he had it.

9

To mend the damage from Evan's visit. I sent him an email saying I'd learned some things about my father that I wanted to share with him and Ian. The spirit of Dave seized me, and I went on to say that these discoveries about my dad had stirred up many emotions, including grief over our conflict and an overwhelming desire to heal the wound, because (here I paused, not wanting to use someone else's words but unable to find better ones) *you and your brother mean more to me than anything in the world.* I also wrote that I couldn't be prouder of him and the work he's doing.

He didn't write back: no surprise. When we visited them at the hospital, though, he made it clear that he'd heard me. We had brought deli sandwiches, and he told me a story as he ate. After they'd cleaned up the baby and put her in a bassinet, she cried pathetically, bleating like a tiny lamb. He went over and touched her hand; she held his index finger and stopped crying. "I can't understand that. How does a newborn baby know enough to calm down just because there's a finger to hold? She couldn't even see me yet."

"I'd call it miraculous," I said.

He had to fly out to Montana again. Ellen and I have spent the last two weekends and many evenings helping out: doing laundry, delivering tubs of my spaghetti sauce, running to the store to buy Lansinoh nipple cream, holding Maya so Erin could shower, and taking her out in the carriage so Erin could nap. I had one useful tip to offer, remembered from thirty years ago: put the baby against your shoulder, lean back against the kitchen counter, and let her spit up straight into the sink after eating. Erin has thanked us effusively after each visit; she's especially grateful, I think, because her mother has a busy life and only flew down from Providence for two days after the baby was born.

I hope the time we've spent with his wife and daughter will connect us to Evan again. If not, at least we've gotten to know our new granddaughter.

With his permission, I made a date for the whole family to crowd into his apartment in Sunset Park and meet the baby. The plan was to use the gathering to report everything I've learned: to deliver a sort of revised eulogy.

They came from three different states: Paul and Judy, Holly, and Ian's whole family. We moved the chairs from the kitchen to the living room and opened a couple of folding chairs from the closet. Wrapped gifts turned the coffee table into a festive little mountain. There was baby equipment everywhere.

We all took turns holding Maya. I read a wordless board book about Carl the dog to Olivia and Daniel, and Sunny took our picture, as always. (She could make a flip book of her children growing up snuggled against me.) Evan hosted almost cordially.

The spirit of the day was so warm and bright, I hesitated to bring up the dead. As soon as Maya went down for a nap, though, Ellen announced, "Dad's been doing some research about Grandpa. You'll all want to hear this."

She said it without a critical undertone. That's progress.

I told them how Grandpa Morris had tried to help German during the war and nine years later. "He stuck his neck out for someone who couldn't defend himself," I said, with a sudden surge of pride. I told them about the arrest and trial, his time in prison, German's fate, and the question of Silvia. Some fussing through the monitor interrupted me and we all paused to listen—Erin gave Evan a *your turn* look—but the noises stopped and Ian urged me to go on. "I've driven to Binghamton, Yonkers, Lebanon, Pennsylvania, and Westport, Connecticut," I said. "Ellen thinks I'm obsessed. But I needed to understand what happened. And I'm glad I did the research. What if we never found out any of this?"

Paul said, "I must be an idiot. I never suspected." Holly was upset that our parents had kept it from us. "What did they think? That we'd suddenly reject them?" I explained what our aunts and uncles had said, that they didn't want us to be traumatized.

Sunny sympathized with Dad: "Maybe he was just ashamed, and didn't want anyone to know." I told her that was exactly what Aunt Ruth had said.

"Poor Grandpa," Ian said. "I can't see him in prison."

"You must have been totally shocked," Evan said.

I told him I'd assumed it was a mistake when I read the first article. "It's still hard to put this together with the person I knew."

"I don't remember any of it," Paul said.

"The police came late at night. You were sleeping."

Ian shook his head. "What a risk to take. Jesus, Grandpa."

I'd brought the contents of Dad's box so they could see the artifacts for themselves. (The pornographic coins stayed home because of Olivia and Daniel.) Evan asked to see the picture of Silvia. After reading the back, he asked what I thought had happened between them. I said I wished I knew.

"If we knew someone in Rome," he said, "they could post the picture on Facebook. Someone might say, 'Hey, that's my grandma.'"

He passed the picture along. Paul had the same thought I did: we might be flooded with messages from scammers claiming to be Dad's illegitimate children and demanding money.

"Or even worse," my sister said, "from the real thing."

"She looks so young," Sunny said. "Maybe she was just a kid who had a crush on him."

Paul estimated that she would be eighty-six or so, if she was still alive.

Judy thought the body language was clear: "She's not just a friend. She has hopes, and he's not sure how to handle it."

"Do we think he told her he was engaged?" Ellen asked.

"Maybe not," Paul said. He had the picture in his hand. "Maybe they fooled around, and now he's going home."

During the quiet that followed, I thought again about the child Dad may have fathered. Paul and Holly may have been thinking the same thing.

"Look at this," Ian said, and showed me the photo. With a

thumbnail, he underlined the ring on Silvia's finger. Was it the one from Dad's box? I couldn't tell for sure—the picture was too small—but maybe, yes. There was a good chance.

"I think you should look for her," Sunny said.

Some things I'd rather not know, I thought.

The doorbell rang while Evan had Maya on his shoulder. A sweaty teenager handed over a big shopping bag. Evan went for his wallet, and I said, "Please."

Unlike every other time I've tried to pay for his meal since he got married, he said, "Okay. Thanks." He barely even scowled.

I set the platter on the kitchen counter and started peeling away the layers of plastic wrap. Before I got halfway, Ellen, Holly, and Judy bustled in and took over. Maya made a tiny whining noise; Evan took bouncing steps to soothe her.

I followed him to the bedroom. Out the window, through the new safety bars, we could see the treetops in the park just beginning to yellow, and the Statue of Liberty.

"How are you doing on sleep?" I asked.

"Not great, but it's worse for Erin. She's a wreck."

I suggested he take a break and let me hold the baby while he had the chance. Head on my shoulder, little body against my chest, bottom supported by one hand: my sleeping granddaughter's warmth came through the swaddling, and stood for the warmth of family, of closeness, which is rare and precious these days.

I remembered handing baby Ian to my father for the first time. My eyes filled with tears. I wandered off and pretended to study the wall safe.

"Did you ever find the combination?"

"No, the old Finns died with the secret."

Quietly—ready to retract the question if he bristled—I asked whether he'd worked out the problem with that interviewee. He said he was going to have to blur the guy's face and alter his voice. Therefore he needed to find more subjects, because no one wants to watch a feature-length blur. Which means more travel. Which means Erin will scream.

Dodging that sore spot, I asked how he had managed to identify white supremacist cops. "Local reporters solicited anonymous tips through Black churches," he said. "But don't tell anyone. If these people find out what we're up to before the film and the articles come out, who knows what they'll try."

He grew talkative, explaining that the FBI did an internal report on the subject in 2006, after scandals in local police departments in L.A., Chicago, Cleveland, and Texas. But they haven't said a word about the issue since. No one knows if they're still paying attention.

I wanted to say, *I know you have to work on your film, I agree it's important, but Maya will only be a baby for a little while. You should spend as much time as you can with her.* If I said it, though, he might snap at me. We had scarcely left the battlefield behind. For the sake of our fragile détente, I swallowed my advice.

While I paced the room with my granddaughter, Evan shared a story about my father. Ian had had to go to the hospital during one of our visits to Florida. (Allergic reaction to Keflex; he couldn't breathe; I'll never forget.) While the rest of us spent the day at the hospital, Grandpa Morris took Evan to the best playground he'd ever seen, with a giant wooden face and hidden passageways. Then they went for ice cream, and watched the parade of boats on the Intra-Coastal Waterway. It was a great day, and he only realized recently that Grandpa was trying to distract him from worrying about his brother, who had left the house wheezing.

"I'm glad you have fond memories of him," I said.

"I have some of you too."

"Really?"

He snorted. "You sound surprised."

I held Maya against me with wide-apart fingers. The warmth spread everywhere.

It's rare that we all eat together. It reminded me of the Sundays when we would pick up my father's elderly parents in Canarsie and take them out for a Chinese dinner in our neighborhood. Before driving to the restaurant, while the kids visited with his parents, Dad would fix a chair with a loose leg, or unclog a drain, or buy groceries for them. I asked my brother and sister if they remembered.

Paul said, "I only remember how it smelled when he sprayed their apartment."

Holly said, "I remember Wayne Wong. They had those round bronze lantern lights."

"Grandma always ordered egg drop soup," I said. "So did I. That was the one thing we had in common."

"And Dad ordered pepper steak," Paul said. "With no onions."

"And then he would drive them home again," I said.

Holly exhaled through pursed lips, as if she still smoked. "Did he ever rest?"

Sunny teaches Spanish at a high school in Queens. I hadn't asked Myriam to translate the second letter from German's mother, so I asked my daughter-in-law. That one was postmarked 1956; Dad would have still been in prison when it arrived.

We had finished lunch and cleaned up, and now we were back in the living room. While Erin nursed Maya, Sunny told us what the letter said.

Dear Morris,
You must have heard what happened to German. This is what you tried to save him from.

There is so much evil in this world, sometimes I think that the devil rules. All his life I feared this. How can God permit such crimes?

My family has changed, it's terrible to see. Marquita has no hope, Oscar fights in school, Elsie stays in her room, she's afraid of everything.

I'm not the same person I was. If I could kill the men who hurt my son, I would do it with my own hands.

And you, you have suffered so much for helping him. We will never forget what you did. May the Lord protect you.
With our gratitude,
Nydia Rosario

One thing more—German mentioned in his letters a guard who was kind to him. I want to thank him but I don't want to call that place, and my son Freddy is too angry. Would you give him our thanks? His name is Chester Carr.

When she got to the end, Sunny handed the letter back with a solemn face.

"Do you think Dad ever relayed the message?" Holly asked.

"I'll try to find out," I said.

Ellen sighed.

❧

It looked as if we might get past the worst of her dissatisfaction without another soul-scraping talk. Driving home from Evan's, though—as I was admiring the lights of downtown from the Brooklyn Bridge—she said, "So when can I expect to see you turn into a fountain of expressed emotion?"

"I was enjoying the day," I said. "I didn't have any reason to curse and scream."

"That covers today."

I did some arithmetic in my head. We've been married for thirty-four years. We met two years before we got married. Since then, she has brought this up in different ways at least ten times. That's an average of once every three and a half years.

"I know there's more inside. Where does it all go?"

What pissed me off about this was that, when I'd finally confronted Evan about his attitude, she accused me of letting *too* much out. But if I pointed out the contradiction, she would criticize me for—I don't know what.

"Okay, so you're not going to turn into a different person. But you could try to show a *little* more."

Two young men in overalls were juggling hammers near City Hall. It was late on a Sunday; only three people were watching. I wished I could stay and watch them perform, by myself.

"I'll tell you what I'm feeling right now: this comes up again and again. You're dissatisfied with me in general. But I thought we had a better marriage than most. So it's upsetting to keep hearing that I've disappointed you."

I watched the jugglers until Ellen said, "The light changed."

She didn't respond to what I'd said until we had crossed Broadway. In the interval, I reflected that it was sad to have fallen into such stereotypical roles. I'm not a cliché in most ways, and neither is she. But here she was, like a complaining wife on an afternoon talk show, pleading her case to a television therapist—*He never opens up with me*—while her husband sat mute, enduring the public humiliation.

"You haven't disappointed me," she said. "You're turning this the wrong way."

I shouted at her: "*WHAT?*"

After a startled flinch, she understood. "Not funny. But at least it's something."

I could have told her about a strong emotion. I could have admitted that the idea of her leaving had scared me to death. But I didn't want to remind her of that option if she had decided against it.

We were in the tunnel, under the Hudson. Somehow it became possible to state my grievance in simple terms.

"I've noticed a pattern," I said. "When Evan has a conflict with me, it's unbearable to you, and you blame me for it. But that's not fair."

She considered my point. When we emerged from the tunnel she said, "You might be right."

I appreciated the concession.

If she retires and changes careers, I may want to do the same. It would only make sense, though, if I could find something satisfying, something significant. Eradicating poverty is more than I can handle. What else could it be?

In movies, lawbreakers seem charismatic and free. In real life, they're greedy, sleazy, and merciless—willing to steal from vulnerable people. To me, anyone who catches crooks like these and brings them to justice is a hero.

It's too late for law school, but the attorney general's office might be willing to hire an older person as an investigator. I should talk to someone.

❧

Yanixa, Myriam's best friend at work, organized a surprise party for her. At five o'clock, ten of us stood in the kitchen in the dark. When Myriam opened the door, Yanixa switched on the light and we shouted, "Happy birthday!"

She snickered at the cake. Printed on the icing was a childhood photo of her, laughing and sticking her tongue out. "How did you even *get* that?" she asked. "I had help," Yanixa said, and Myriam's mother stepped out from the other side of the refrigerator, followed by Myriam's husband and baby.

"Help Mommy blow out the candles," she said, taking her daughter in her arms. Alissa surveyed the room imperiously.

Myriam's mother carefully transferred the photo to a plate before cutting the cake. Myriam handed Alissa off to her husband (who's built like a small football player, with blue eyes and thick, vertical hair) and served slices to all of us.

She looked pretty in her magenta blouse and black pants. I didn't want to be caught staring, so I turned to read the easel announcements. My turn to buy the coffee pods is coming up soon.

She introduced me to her family as she handed me my cake. They knew my name. Her husband works for the Knicks; he shook my hand with a muscular grip and said, "I hear you're a good boss." Her mother—who's ten years younger than I am and wears a lot of makeup, but can't conceal the deep creases in her face—stopped slicing to say, "Thank you for the support you give her."

"She's an exceptional person. You did a great job raising her."

Once everyone had cake, Myriam's mother pulled me aside. "At her other job, they put too much pressure on her. All they gave was criticism. But you give her praise. You help with suggestions. It makes so much difference."

She spoke emphatically, holding my gaze. I asked if she still worked. She told me she had been a pharmacist in Beirut, and managed to re-establish herself in Buenos Aires, but by the time they came here, she was too old to start again. She works with her sister now, importing scarves and jewelry.

I said, "Thank you for telling me what you told me. I think very highly of your daughter."

She squeezed my arm as if we were family.

People left once they'd finished their cake. I watched Myriam hug each of them in turn. What could I do, except wish her all the happiness in the world?

The Federal Bureau of Prisons website informed me that they take twenty to thirty working days to respond to inquiries. I doubted they would have current contact information anyway. And if they did, they wouldn't share it with me.

I found a mention of the guard's name in a 2007 obituary. Nell Carr of Rome, Georgia, had only two surviving relatives, her children, Darlene and Chester.

One other search result also matched: a newspaper photo of two men on ladders, working at a Habitat for Humanity site ten years ago. The caption identified the thin one in the baseball cap, face in shadow, as Chester Carr.

I dialed the number listed for him in Rome. Imagining how it would feel to pick up the phone and hear a message like this one, I smiled.

"Mm-hm," a papery voice said.

I asked if this was Chester Carr, who used to work at the penitentiary in Atlanta.

Many seconds passed before he mumbled, "Yes."

Realizing that retired prison guards might sometimes receive threats, I explained that I was calling to relay a thank you from a former prisoner's mother.

That made no difference. "Uh-huh."

I asked if he remembered an inmate named German Rosario.

Because of what had happened, I assumed he would remember instantly. He hesitated, though. Finally, he mumbled a single faint syllable. "Yes."

I told him what Nydia Rosario's letter had said. "I don't know if my father ever conveyed the message."

"No, he didn't."

There was no accusation in his voice, only wary reserve. I couldn't understand why Dad hadn't honored the request. It didn't seem like him.

Ellen appeared in my office doorway in underwear and T-shirt. "Can you—"

I pointed to the phone in my hand. She asked with her eyebrows, *Who?* I shook my head and turned away.

Carr had nothing to say about the message from Nydia. I told him that the letter had only reached me a few weeks ago, and that I hadn't gotten it translated until yesterday.

His silence was hard for me to understand.

"I saw the picture of you working with Habitat for Humanity. Have you met Jimmy Carter?"

"One time, mm-hm."

With that, I gave up. I apologized for bothering him, and he said mildly, "That's all right."

Ellen had no theory to offer about his reticence. She asked if I would walk to Duane Reade and pick up her prescription, because she had already gotten undressed.

It was a breezy, warm night. Men in suits were still getting off the PATH, coming home late, lifting their eyes to the darkening sky. Along with Ellen's Fosamax, I bought a small container of coffee Häagen-Dazs to share with her.

The call came when I was a block from home.

"This is Chester Carr," he said. "Is this an all right time?"

He spoke softly, with an accent I only hear when politicians from the deep South appear on the news. I hadn't noticed before because he'd said so little.

He explained that he'd left that job right after Rosario died.

"Was it because of what happened?"

"Yes, sir."

That raised some questions. *Did you consider him a friend? Did other guards witness the beating and let it continue?*

"I never told anyone how he really died. It wasn't like they said."

I thought the connection was failing, but the clicks turned out to be Carr suppressing his own crying.

By then I had reached our building. I kept going down Grove Street and turned on Mercer, where it was quieter.

"If it's hard to talk about, you could start somewhere else. You said you quit after that?"

He told me his entire work history. At first he didn't know how he would earn a living. A new GE factory opened nearby and he took a job there, making transformers. After that he worked in home construction. Finally he went back to school and became a physical therapist. He worked at the Floyd Medical Center for almost thirty years.

I said he must have been a young man when he worked at the prison. "Twenty-two," he said. "I never should have set foot in that place."

"Why is that?"

"It changes you. The cons hate you and you hate them."

I didn't comment, though I had questions. I was afraid he might hang up at the slightest nudge.

"I couldn't stop what happened. I tried, but I couldn't."

I gave him time to collect himself. He seemed to have run into a stone wall.

"You said you hated the prisoners. But German said you were good to him."

"He wasn't like the rest. He kept to himself. I thought he might be dangerous. Then they assigned me to censor mail. I saw the letters he wrote home. Most prisoner letters are pathetic, some of them can hardly write the alphabet, but he sounded like a normal, respectable person."

You couldn't befriend an inmate, Carr explained. That was the first thing they taught you. But he noticed German reading a book about horses once, and asked about it.

German said he might look for a job working with animals when he got out.

A while after that, Carr noticed a horse magazine in the pile at the barber shop, and asked if he could take it. He placed the magazine next to German's motor in the electrical shop.

That was it—the sum total of his kindness to German—which was why it surprised him to hear that German had mentioned him.

"You said that what happened wasn't what they reported."

Silence. A young couple passed me, sharing a pretzel.

"Most of the guards were all right," Carr said. "One of them, though—he was nasty and stupid. They never assigned him to make the count because he couldn't come up with the right number. And he gave German a hard time. He acted like he was just kidding, but he kept poking."

"You mean with comments?"

"Or his baton. We weren't supposed to carry a baton, but he would sometimes. There were a lot of incidents."

He stopped. I waited.

"One time German was waxing the aisle with the machine and L.K. came up behind him and jabbed him in the back with his stick. Said he was blocking traffic. German asked him, 'Why do you keep bothering me?'"

L.K. ended up accusing German of hiding something. He told him to show both hands. Then he said to turn them over, and smashed both hands at once with his baton.

The blow broke a couple bones. Whatever German said at the infirmary, no disciplinary action followed.

Carr was taking so long to tell his story, I worried that my phone would run out of power. "Does that have something to do with how he died?"

"It does."

The little container of ice cream in the bag kept banging against my leg as I walked.

"I got the story later, from the other prisoners. L.K. asked German if he had any contraband. 'Any Spanish girly magazines? Any señoritas?' It was just an excuse to shake down the cell and throw German's things around. When he turned up that magazine, the one I gave him, he asked if German had a thing for horses—if he liked screwing things with four legs.

He wouldn't let it go. He said, 'I asked you a question. You go around screwing animals?' And German finally said, 'No. Do you?'"

The tidy row houses, the lush little gardens behind their iron railings, the black Lab puppy tugging at its leash: everything around me magnified the dread.

"The cell block was howling. I came to see what was going on. 'L.K. screws animals!' That's what they were yelling. He couldn't give up his authority like that. So he cracked German on the head and dragged him out of the cell."

I wanted the story to end differently than I knew it would. I wanted German to come out alive.

Carr cleared his throat. "I'm not sure I can do this."

"Is the point that L.K. beat him to death? Not the other prisoners?"

"It's worse than that."

I couldn't guess what he meant.

He calmed himself with audible breaths. "I followed them to the break room. A couple other guards were there. One was the man who trained me, Melvin Barton. He was over fifty, he carried pictures of his grandchildren in his wallet. I figured he would calm L.K. down."

Why didn't he? I wondered. He should have.

"German tried to tell his side. They didn't even look up. Barton was eating plums and reading the paper, and Tillson had a comic book. L.K. made German stand spread-eagled with his hands against the wall. Barton said, 'Do what you're gonna do and take him out of here.' So L.K. took out a sap from his pocket—"

"A what?"

"A sap. A blackjack. They're illegal, but some of the guards kept them for self-defense."

I remembered a picture from some old comic strip, probably Dick Tracy: a bad guy with a black eye mask, in profile, gritting his teeth and raising what looked like a skinny yellow kidney bean, drawn with perpendicular cross hatching.

"German kept looking over his shoulder, he saw what was

coming. When L.K. lifted his arm, German turned and put his fist in L.K.'s gut. He was small, he looked wild and scared, but he knocked L.K. off his feet."

I had to sit down. The stoops all had fences guarding them, so I crossed the street and sat on the rounded steps of number 55. The stone was damp and cold.

"The other guards must have stepped in at that point."

"Mm-hm. German was bent over, in pain—that punch messed up his hand again, I think—but they went after him like he was a mad dog, like he'd kill us all if they didn't pound him into the ground."

I had to ask. "Couldn't you stop them?"

His voice cracked. "I froze. I couldn't even talk, at first."

He sounded ashamed.

"Did L.K. join in?"

"Not right away. He was on the floor, trying to catch his breath."

I thought we'd reached the end, but there was more.

"These were normal men, Barton and Tillson. They had families. But it's like a switch got thrown. They just kept clubbing him."

The incident was so remote in time, hearing about it was like viewing black-and-white photographs of an atrocity. The crime called for anger, but I could only muster sorrow.

At a certain point, German looked up at Carr. It was only a glance, before he closed his eyes. "He gave up on me. That's what got me. I screamed at them—'That's enough!'"

"Did they stop?"

"They did. They just stood there panting. And chuckling, kind of."

Maybe they would have listened if you'd jumped in sooner. "So it wasn't L.K. who killed him."

"I'm not finished. After they stopped, L.K. stood up."

I thought I might pass out. I let my head hang lower.

"You couldn't see any blood on German, or bruising. They only hit him where his shirt and pants would cover it. He was on his back with his eyes closed. Only his hands were moving, like trying to reach something and hold on."

Carr took a few shallow breaths.

"I didn't think L.K. would do more than spit on him. I said, 'Let him be.' He said, 'I will.' And then he stomped on German's chest, like you would to break a two-by-four. He said, 'You shoulda stayed in your own country.' Then he stomped on German's face."

The parked car in front of me had a Colorado license plate, with the snowy peaks above the numbers and letters. I put myself there: at high altitude, far from here, far from the past and German Rosario.

Carr wrapped up his account. The other guards turned on L.K., they called him a dumb so-and-so and a lot of other things. They planned a cover-up and threatened Carr if he didn't go along. Even Barton, the grandfather, told him he had no choice.

German was still breathing, a horrible whistle. Carr said he wanted to take him to the infirmary. They wouldn't let him.

L.K. put German back in his cell after lights out. He died before the morning count. The autopsy said internal bleeding. When the investigators questioned Carr, he said the fight must have happened on his supper break, because he hadn't seen or heard it.

I think he hoped I would say, *You did the best you could.* But I couldn't say it. I kept thinking he should have done more.

"It's like a nightmare I never stopped having."

I asked why he never told anyone the truth. There was a reason. He was still living with his parents; L.K. came by the next day and took him out on the front lawn. He swore if Carr ever breathed a word, he'd burn down the house and everyone in it.

I thought of Oscar, and what the story would do to him. He wouldn't hear it from me.

"What happened to the prisoners they blamed it on?" I asked.

"Three went on trial, but two agreed to testify against one."

"Didn't the investigators talk to the other prisoners? The ones who saw L.K. drag him out of his cell?"

"I don't know what they did. All I know is, they convicted the one."

I reminded myself of the pressure the other guards had put on Carr. I've never faced anything like it.

"They were all convicted murderers," he said. "It wasn't that bad of an injustice."

"Did they execute him?"

"No, they just added some time to his sentence."

That man deserves to have his name cleared, I thought. Even if he's dead, his family should know.

"I've spent my whole life trying to make amends," Carr said.

"Are the other guards still alive?"

"Only Tillson, last I looked. He was in a nursing home. But that was a few years ago."

"You ought to tell a newspaper what really happened."

I realized before he answered why he wouldn't do what I'd suggested. Aside from allowing the other guards to beat a prisoner to death, he had taken part in a sixty-year cover-up. He would end his life in disgrace.

"I'm sorry," he said.

I couldn't push. If he told the story publicly, Oscar would hear how his father had died, in detail.

"I've repented in my heart," Carr said.

I didn't doubt his sincerity. Much as I wished I could extract some remnant of justice from all this brutality, I didn't want to hurt him.

"I took a risk by talking to you," he said. "You won't use it against me, will you?"

"I won't."

He coughed weakly, a dry, raspy cough. "I better go now," he said.

Before he hung up, I said, "You should talk to your minister. It might help more than talking to me."

He hesitated. "Maybe."

He won't do it. Like my father, he'll keep his secret from his family until he dies.

I found myself on a stranger's stoop, a block and a half from home. For a confused moment, I forgot that German wasn't a relative. I saw him spread-eagled against the wall, turning to look over his shoulder, afraid but also enraged.

A search for the phrase *convicted of killing German Rosario* led me to a single article. Two of the defendants had testified that they acted as lookouts. William Gentle had been sentenced to five additional years in prison.

If I were Oscar, I would want to know who really killed my father. But if I tell him, he'll ask to speak to Carr.

I left the stoop and walked toward home. The street was quiet and still. In the middle of the roadway, a baby's undershirt lay flat, a dim, soiled little ghost.

10

Aren't you supposed to wait a year for the unveiling?" Evan asked.

We were driving from the hotel to the cemetery, with our carry-on bags in the trunk.

"That's a custom, not a law," Ellen said.

"You know Charlotte," I said. "She moves fast."

We passed many palm trees and a bus stop bench with an ad for a Christmas store on its backrest, partly masked by a local candidate's bumper sticker. Ian said, "I used to like coming here to visit. But it looks so flat and empty now."

"That's how it always looked to me," I said.

At the airport the night before, as we'd emerged from the jetway, the blast of humidity had sent me back to the years before I met Ellen, when I would find Dad waiting at the gate, searching for my face. I kept tugging my suitcase behind me, and told no one about the crushing pressure in my chest.

Young men were digging some kind of ditch by the side of the road. Only half of them wore shirts. A foreign visitor might have said, *They look like slaves*.

"Grandpa used to call Black people 'colored,'" Evan said. "You mentioned that in the eulogy."

"It's what he grew up with. To him it was respectful." But my stomach would tighten when he said it.

Just before we reached the cemetery, we passed the entrance to Loxahatchee. I had dragged my father there many times. Mostly we saw waterfowl, which I identified with my Peterson's guide. (A small flock of gallinules: unmistakable, the red of their bills extending all the way up their foreheads.) We only spotted an alligator once, far off and sleeping.

Aunt Ruth's right arm was in a sling. Charlotte, in a loose plum top with a black-and-teal silk scarf, had hold of Ruth's other forearm. They were chatting vigorously. Charlotte's hair is light copper now, short and tousled, with bangs that sweep to one side. I believe Jane Fonda wears her hair similarly.

Irv was there, and Sam (with a new health aide), and Paul and Holly, and Charlotte's brother, sister, and daughter, and the young rabbi who had conducted the funeral service. Irv explained that Ruth had tripped on a curb and broken her wrist in two places. "She's lucky that's all she broke," he said. "I call her the Iron Lady."

Sam had spent two weeks in the hospital with pneumonia. He'd lost weight since last time, and his cheeks hung slack.

As the rabbi recited in Hebrew, I held Ellen's hand. Ian's shoulder pressed against mine; Evan stood close behind me. The words *It's over* kept running through my head. The word *it's* encompassed many things: my father's life… his years in the wheelchair… the troubles he'd hid from us… my last chance to speak to him.

At the foot of the grave, lower than the grass and neatly covered by a gauzy cloth, lay my father's stone. When the rabbi finished his prayers, he removed the cloth and revealed the inscription Charlotte had composed: *Loving Husband, Father, Brother, and Grandfather*. She had chosen the words to mirror the ones on Mom's stone—a wise and diplomatic decision. The new letters looked knife-sharp.

(Dad and Charlotte had both bought joint plots years ago with their first spouses. After they married, they agreed it would be wasteful to leave them unused. This must happen often.)

What could we have put on his footstone if we'd wanted to pay him a more specific tribute? Back in August, I would have referred to his popularity. If *"no man is poor who has friends,"* then *Morris was a wealthy man*. I'd go in a different direction now. *More noble than we knew*. Or simply, *A beautiful heart*.

Paul, Holly, and I stayed by the grave for a few minutes after the others had gone back to their cars. None of us spoke, but it was good to stand there together.

Paul hugged us both and left. Holly followed soon after. I lingered.

The sky was overcast, sunless. A hawk crossed overhead in a straight line, beating its wings. Nearby, a tree shaded a stone bench. I had come here twice to visit Mom's grave with Ellen, and we had sat on that bench to get out of the sun. The tree had grown much wider since then.

To honor my father, I searched for a memory that would do him justice, and found this one: when we first moved back to Queens, he used to take us to the tiny amusement parks near our apartment—Kiddy City on Northern Boulevard, McGinnis on Jericho Turnpike. I loved those places. I loved the Scrambler, and the roller coasters. He watched us go around and around, smiling placidly, enjoying our pleasure. One time, on the helicopter ride—you pulled the bar to go up and pushed it to go down—I was still all the way up when the ride ended. The operator couldn't bring me down unless I pushed the bar (at least, that's how I remember it) and I liked being up there too much to come down voluntarily. Exasperated, the man told Dad to make me cooperate. Dad called up to me, chuckling, "Come on, Kenny, cut it out."

No one was nearby, no one could see my face, but I put my hand over it, a visor from eyes to mouth, to hide what was happening there.

A friend of Charlotte's had set up the deli platters on the dinner table. There were fewer platters than in August, and fewer people.

We segregated ourselves, Dad's family in the living room, Charlotte's group in the kitchen. I told Ruth, Irv, and Sam some of what I'd learned. When I explained how Dad had given German first aid and carried him to safety, Ruth said, "I'm not at all surprised." Sam was too dazed to take it in.

Irv told the story of how Dad met Mom, which I had never heard. "He had to steal her away from my friend Max. We went to Coney Island, Ruth and me and Rozzie and Max, and your father came along. Max threw your mother in the water—he thought it was funny, but she couldn't swim and she started screaming, even though it was only up her knees. After that she just wanted to get away from him, so she went to the boardwalk for custard and Morris went with her. That was it for Max."

Holly asked what ever happened to Max, and Irv said, "He ran a black-car service, for lawyers and whatnot. He lives a few miles from here—I still have lunch with him sometimes. But he's a jerk. He always was. Worst parent in the world. His kids won't even talk to him."

"But you stayed friends with him," Ruth said ruefully.

Irv shrugged. "He calls me. What am I gonna do?"

Ellen gave my hand a little squeeze, which I returned.

The reminiscing turned to Mom. When she was in a good mood, she used to sing. Holly remembered her singing "Somewhere" from *West Side Story*. I remembered her singing "I Loved You Once in Silence" while doing the dishes. When she couldn't remember the lyrics, she filled in with *la la la*s.

A car pulled up outside, a silver Mercedes. A stout, white-haired man in a red polo shirt and iridescent sunglasses came up the path with a box of Saran wrap in his hand. He apologized as he passed through—"Sorry, she asked me to bring this"—and went straight to the kitchen.

I'd never seen him before, but I already suspected how he fit into the picture.

Because it was possible that I'd never be here again, I wandered through the house, just looking around. In the guest room, next to Dad's computer, one framed snapshot remained: Paul, Holly, and I stood with our arms around each other, in front of a lighthouse on Cape Cod. We took that trip when I was eight. All I remember from it is running off a beach as flies bit us.

I brought the picture to the kitchen, to ask Charlotte if I could take it with me. She was telling her sister and brother and friends about travel plans. "We want to go on a cruise but we can't agree: I want to see Greece and Croatia, he wants to go to Israel." The man who'd brought the Saran wrap said, "I've never seen Israel. I want to go while I can still walk." But Charlotte has been to Israel twice and craves something different. "I need to see something new," she said.

"Why don't you do your trip first," her daughter said, "and Bob's trip six months later?"

"Queen Solomon," Bob called her.

"You deserve it," said one of the friends.

Bob seemed friendly and pleasant, but slightly moronic. His hair swooped down toward the center of his forehead in a bell curve, stiffened by hairspray. He may be smarter than he seemed, if he ended up in a Mercedes—unless the money came from his previous wife.

I tried to back away unseen, but Charlotte said, "Wait, Kenny, I have something for you."

She led me to the bedroom. On the way, she said, "I don't want you to think, because I met someone, that I didn't adore your father. I did. But it's hard to be alone."

"I can appreciate that," I said.

From an otherwise empty drawer in my father's dresser, she took a box that had once held a hundred sheets of Ilford photo paper. She'd found it in the garage. Inside were eight-by-ten black-and-white portraits of Dad's friends and relatives. A perfect quarter-inch border framed each picture; the edges curled upwards slightly. Here were Uncle Sam and Aunt Phoebe in front of their pool; Ruth and Irv by the birdbath in their garden; Snow Weiss and Betty sitting in the open back of their station wagon; and many others, most of whom I didn't recognize. Judging by their haircuts and ages, I'd say he took the pictures in the early sixties, soon after we moved back to Queens. What made them interesting was that he seemed to have told jokes to his subjects just before pressing the shutter release. Each person reacted differently. Charlie Feldstein let out a wide-mouthed guffaw. Uncle Sam's eyes closed down to slits. Hank Finkel grinned uncertainly, pretending he got the joke while trying to figure it out. Ruth and Irv glanced at each other, sharing a laugh with gleaming eyes. Goldie (a widow, pre-Julius) tossed her head back.

Beneath the stack of photos were strips of negatives in

glassine sleeves. My father may only have been an amateur, but the portraits capture a lot. I think I'll get the ones of my aunts and uncles printed professionally. Paul and Holly may want copies, too.

"They're all yours," Charlotte said.

He had stopped using the darkroom around the time that Mom died. I asked Charlotte if he'd had any other hobbies, besides bowling, and she said, "He was always finding something new. He brewed beer for a while. We played golf. He learned chess. He volunteered, setting up medical alert systems in old people's houses."

I'd known about the beer and the golf, but not the chess or the volunteering.

They'd had different interests—hers were gambling, Mah Jongg, and folk art—and had pursued them separately. The arrangement worked well. They never seemed less than contented. But, as Aunt Goldie once observed (in front of Julius, to my horror), "A second marriage isn't like the first." Living with Charlotte was much easier on Dad than living with Mom, but it looked more like companionship than love.

She had cleaned out his closet, including the many pairs of sneakers and shoes that used to stand on the floor rack, toes up. There was no folded newspaper on his night table. (Paperback mysteries were piled on hers, as always.) Other than his lamp and clock, all that remained was a gold tie bar. That surprised me, because I hadn't seen Dad wear a tie in years. The tie bar was monogrammed, with the letters *RL* in script—baffling, until I thought of the name *Robert*.

Bob may have known Charlotte and my father for years. Maybe he's had his eye on her ever since Dad's stroke. She's the most attractive of her crowd, by far. Charlotte may have known he was interested.

He didn't waste time. But I can't call him a vulture. At their age, it would have been foolish to let months pass for the sake of appearances.

Charlotte's friend had said, *You deserve it,* and she was right. My father's stroke had turned his wife into a prisoner. She couldn't dance, she couldn't travel. Everything that gave her joy had been put out of reach.

It must have tortured Dad: to be a burden, an obstacle, after doing everything for everyone all his life.

I wish I'd spent more time with him these last few years. But we had trouble finding things to talk about. (If he'd let me in on his secrets, we could have talked forever.)

Charlotte has every right to move on. She took care of him loyally after his stroke, and never complained, at least not in front of me. She's a bird, and Dad's infirmity chained her to the ground. Now she'll fly again. I can't begrudge her that.

An attack of heartburn struck soon after we left Dad's development. I pulled into the CVS just south of Atlantic.

While standing in line to pay for Rolaids, I recognized the old man in front of me. "Snow?"

I had to say it again, louder.

His head sat lower on his shoulders than before, and jutted forward, as if it were attached directly to his sternum. White stubble, like sandpaper, covered his chin, lip, and jawline. His eyelids were very red.

He shook my hand and asked what the hell I was doing there. Embarrassed, I explained that I'd just come from the unveiling, and that Charlotte had only invited family. "Don't worry about it," he said. "I've been to enough."

He was holding a box of Depends and a Milky Way bar. He saw me glance at the candy bar and swore—eyes swinging left and right—that it was for Betty.

We shook hands again after he paid the cashier. "Okay, take it easy," he said.

"Stay healthy," I replied: one of the more awkward comments I've made in recent years.

I found him waiting for me just inside the exit. "Kenny, I've been meaning to call you."

He looked distressed. "You asked me a question, and I didn't think Morris would want me to answer it. But I keep feeling like you ought to know. *Someone* should know."

I had no idea what he was talking about.

"That girl in the picture…"

He wiped his lips with the back of his hand and stretched his neck like Rodney Dangerfield. Based on the introduction, I could guess the gist.

"What a guy does when he's young, his kids shouldn't come down too hard on him for it."

Two different women came to mind, women I should never have gone out with. I'd told myself to give them a chance, but knew there was no way I'd stay with them long-term. They both considered me cruel in the end.

"He was all torn up when he came home. He didn't know if he should marry your mother or send for the girl."

"He told you this?"

"Me and nobody else. He was confused. He was obsessed with her. I told him, 'You don't really know her.' They could hardly talk to each other with the language thing, right? And she was Catholic—there's so much they didn't have in common. He would have been crazy to marry a girl from Italy. That's what I told him."

"Did he say if he slept with her?"

"He never said the words. But I knew."

The evidence seemed strong to me too. "I've been wondering if I might have a half-brother or sister over there."

"I don't know the answer to that one. He got some letters from her, but he never said anything."

If not for Snow, Dad might have sent for Silvia and married her. I'm not sure how they could have overcome the differences.

I thanked him for telling me. He said, "I hope I did the right thing. But who knows?"

How many times, when Mom sank into her black depths, did Dad think of Silvia? When he stared at the kitchen wall, was he seeing that teenage face and the dark curls around it?

❦

My sons shared a cab with us from the airport to Jersey City. We dropped them at the PATH and got out for hugs. "I love you, Dad," Ian said. Evan squeezed my shoulder.

"Thank you both for coming," I said. "I'm glad you were there."

I kissed them both on the cheek, and they went down the escalator together. At the back of Evan's head, I could see a circle of scalp through the thin hair. That was a shock. I didn't start losing hair there until a couple years ago.

But it's all right. My boys have wives and children now, and work they care about. It wasn't always that way. I used to worry every time we parted, *How will they live?* Especially Evan: how would he find a companion and survive at a job when he lashed out at every minor irritation?

This is one of the good times. I should remind myself of that, every day.

❦

My knees ached from sitting on the plane. It was a warm night for January, so after unpacking, Ellen and I walked to the water-front to stretch our legs.

"I was thinking about gravestones," I told her. "They may have evolved from those rocks they used to use to seal up tombs. Maybe the idea was, you don't want the dead climbing out and complicating the lives of the living. But a footstone doesn't do the job. It's not much of a barrier—it's just a label."

Ellen had nothing to say to that. She just whistled: "I Whistle a Happy Tune."

At the pier, we went all the way to the far railing, as close to Manhattan as you can get. A ferry chugged away from us, churning water behind it. The tail of a helicopter blinked red as it flew downriver.

"I worry about my parents," Ellen said. "I'm so afraid of getting that call."

"I'll tell you how it works. You have no control over it. The call comes, and you get through it."

Restless flecks of brown, gray, and black rippled below us. I had told Ellen on the plane what Snow told me about Silvia, but I hadn't told her how the story had affected me.

"I wish I could find her, if she's still alive," I said. "I know it's irrational."

"I doubt she'd be happy to hear from you."

"Probably not. But still."

We watched the lights move on the water.

"You have two choices," she said. "You can let it go. Or you could send the picture to those people we met in Rome last year. I'm Facebook friends with her."

The offer surprised me. "Would you think I was foolish if I did that?"

She deliberated. "Not exactly."

We seemed to have gotten past our crisis. I worried that she would remember her dissatisfactions, though, if I got us embroiled in some unnecessary debacle.

On the way home, the wind blew in our faces. She took my arm, snugly.

I depend on her in so many ways. When things go wrong at work, she lets me explain and complain, and brings me a glass of wine, and massages my head like a sixties sitcom wife, which she's anything but. When friends invite us somewhere and I'd rather stay home, she pulls me out of my too-comfortable chair and keeps me from turning into an old recluse.

Her ankle turned on a cobblestone as we crossed the light-rail tracks. I reached with my free hand to grab the arm that had lost hold of mine. "Good catch," she said.

We do this for each other, I thought. We save each other from damaging falls. It's instinctive.

But that's not why I need her. I need her for a much simpler reason. *In the end we're just walking each other home*, a famous guru once wrote. I can't say it better than that. We're walking together, to the end, so that neither of us has to walk the road alone.

(He meant something different, I know, something more spiritual and metaphoric, but I prefer my simple interpretation. It means more to me.)

Emiliana, the woman we met in the restaurant on our vacation last year, posted the photo with a note in Italian. *Do you recognize this woman? Her name is Silvia and she would be 86 years old now. If you know her, please comment below.*

I didn't expect anything to come of it—nearly three million people live in Rome—but Emiliana is an extraordinarily friendly woman (that's why we ended up chatting with her and driving around Rome in her tiny car with her and her husband) and I thought that, perhaps, among her many friends and acquaintances, someone would know Silvia's face.

No such message has arrived. I did have a dream, though, in which Silvia's daughter asked her mother questions and sent me a long, detailed email (which then became a letter, and then a face-to-face conversation), reporting what she had learned: that her mother never found the love she wanted, that her parents' marriage was not a happy one, that Morris was a bad man, a liar. "He promised he would marry her, but he never did. Thank God they didn't make a baby!" As far as the daughter was concerned, justice had finally been done, because now Morris's family knew what he'd done to her mother.

It was only a dream, but I imagine that a conversation with an actual daughter of Silvia's might go in a similar direction.

Among the bills and fundraising letters in the mail, there's a letter for Ellen from the New York Botanical Garden's School of Professional Horticulture, a packet of press releases from the New York State Attorney General's Criminal Enforcement and Financial Crimes Bureau (I had lunch with someone there—a job may be possible), and a small manila envelope from Oscar Rosario, who wrote me a note and folded it around a smaller envelope. *I found this in my mother's things. Your Father went through rough times. I didn't know that. He's still a hero to us. —Your friend, Oscar.*

The inner envelope, with a three-cent stamp, is addressed to Mrs. Nydia Rosario. My father put his initials on the rear flap, with his address on Sixty-Third Drive, Rego Park, N.Y.

Dear Mrs. Rosario,

I'm sorry it took so long to answer your letter. My wife sent me a translation, but I didn't want the prison censors to read my letter to you.

I just came home last week. No, no one told me about German until you did. I wish I knew what to say. They should never have put him in prison. He didn't belong there.

This is a bad time for me, too. The worst in my life. I'm staying with my sister because my wife thinks it's upsetting the kids to have me back. The littlest one is scared of me. He keeps hiding and when his brother tells him it's okay, that's Daddy, he says, "I don't know him." My wife said it was easier when I was gone.

She should be helping, not blaming me. Sometimes I think I married the wrong person.

It might have been a mistake to walk out, but I didn't know what else to do. I don't have a way to support my family. I might try moving somewhere new and sending them money. My sister says that's crazy but I'm not so sure. Roz is still young, she could start over.

My wife's state of mind is fragile. I can't say these things to her. I don't want to tell my sister all the details, either. I'm sorry about pouring it all out to you, especially after everything you've gone through. No parent should have to suffer what you suffered.

I will always remember German. He was a good man. That day in Italy, while we waited for it to get dark, he faced the situation bravely—more than I would have.

You might like to know about a certain memory I have of him. Whenever we had to unload the mules, I would see him lay his hand on the side of the mule's head. They always looked peaceful when he did that.

Here is something else you should keep in mind: he made it home from the war, he got married and had a family. For a while everything was good. And he left something behind: his kids, and the people who loved him.

I send you all of my sympathy,
Morris Weintraub

He wrote these words and folded this page, down the middle and then in thirds. Almost sixty years ago, he handled this piece of paper.

It was hard for Mom when he got out, Ruth said. She must have been thinking about the days when he stayed with her. Goldie said Mom almost left him.

The littlest one is scared of me.

The only light I've switched on is the sconce by the front door. The white page shines against the black dinner table.

I should take my coat off.

I searched, and kept searching. I suppose this is what I was looking for.

On the table, a cookbook sits on top of the newspapers. Two daffodils have begun to fade in their narrow vase. This is my home, but we've only lived here a few years. The place doesn't mean much to me—not like the house where we raised our sons, or the home I grew up in.

Toward the end of the letter, as deep in despair as he was, he remembered this woman's grief. He tried to give her something to hold onto.

"That's Daddy." "I don't know him." There isn't much I can do about that now.

What do I want? I'm not sure, but whatever it is, I can't have it.

No—I do know what I want. I want him to walk through the door so I can put my arms around him and smell his stale-skin-and-cigarettes smell. I want to tell him, *Listen, Dad. I know what you did for German. It wasn't foolish. It wasn't a mistake. I admire you for it. More than you can imagine.*

ACKNOWLEDGMENTS

Many people—friends and strangers—generously answered my questions, enabling me to put flesh on what began as the thinnest of skeletons.

But before I name them, I'd like to thank Bill Lee, whose many editorial suggestions made this a much better book. (And this isn't the first time he's done that.)

Special thanks to Chuck Genco for sharing his stories and memories, and to Brian Graham-Jones for spending so much time on the phone explaining his work to me.

Others who answered the call when I needed information include: Ann Brown, Mike Emmerich, Matt Wolf, Bob Goodman, Marsha Rosoff, Peter Wolk, James Franklin, Joe Bleshman, Gary Friedland, Ira Cure, Howard Cure, Nina Boire, Maya Scherer, Morris Fostoff, Bernie Holst, Gary Alden, Mara Daniel, Adam Freedman, Caroline at the NYC Bar Association Library, James Bleshman, Sharon Day, Kevin Crutchfield, and Jerry Weiss.

To give credit where credit where credit is due: when my wife read this book in manuscript form, she scribbled at the bottom of one paragraph, *Ellen sighed.* The sentence was perfect, so I kept it. Thank you, Jennifer.

Heartfelt thanks, too, to Jaynie Royal and Pam Van Dyk for putting my work out into the world. You are an impressive team, and I'm grateful.

Finally, thank you to Eyal Press, author of *Beautiful Souls,* the book that planted the seed for this one.